DEATH TO THE HIGHEST BIDDER

NICOLE ELLIS

DEATH TO THE HIGHEST BIDDER

By Nicole Ellis

For the Erickson family.

Without your boathouse, there wouldn't have been a Jill Andrews series. Thank you for the inspiration and a lifetime of happy memories spent with all of you at the beach.

1

"*J*ill, did you hear what I said?" Nancy Davenport's eyes drilled into me as she paced the floor of the main room at my in-laws' business, the Boathouse Event Center.

I looked up from the notepad that I'd been furiously scribbling on. "Yes, I heard you." I turned the paper around to show her. "See?"

I almost felt like sticking out my tongue at her. Something about her made me want to act like my three-year-old son, Mikey. If Nancy wasn't so entrenched as a volunteer at the Busy Bees Preschool, I'd never have taken this much guff from her, but I didn't want there to be any ill effects on Mikey.

She waved her hand at me. "I can't make out any of your chicken scratch on there. Please make sure the coverings on the round tables are red and the tablecloths on the buffet table are blue. An Americana look will be perfect for the auction's aviation theme."

I gritted my teeth. "Of course. We can definitely do that." I'd already changed the tablecloth colors five times, according to her whim of the week. We'd gone through an elegant silver and black, a stately navy and white, and several other color combinations. The preschool auction was only ten days away, and I hoped she'd make a final decision soon. Our linen supplier was forgiving, but soon we'd need to lock in our choices.

"And did we talk about the arrangement for the stage? There needs to be room for some of the larger auction items and a podium for the auctioneer."

"Yes, of course." I jotted down her request, mainly for her benefit as I'd already heard it several times and made a note in my computer files.

After thirty more minutes of demands, Nancy finally left and I settled down at my desk to work.

After checking and double-checking that every detail of the auction was on track, I rubbed my eyes and closed the lid on my laptop. Who'd have thought organizing a preschool auction would take so much time? My sister-in-law Desi had warned me. I should have listened to her. Then again, it might not have been too bad if Nancy Davenport hadn't been involved.

"Jill?" My mother-in-law, Beth, poked her head into my windowless office.

I looked up. "Hey." I rubbed my eyes again, trying to make there only be one of her in my line of sight. If I didn't get out of there soon, I would be a walking zombie.

"You're still here? I thought you went home hours ago. I came in to close up shop for the night." She leaned against the door frame, scrutinizing me. "You look awful. Is everything going ok with the auction?"

"Thanks, Beth." I attempted to mock-glare at her, but even that took too much energy for me to pull off. "Yeah, it's fine. I just have a lot to do, and Nancy keeps changing her mind about what she wants."

"Well, we're letting them have the auction here for a substantial discount. Tell her she's getting what she's getting. If she's not happy with that, she can go somewhere else next year."

"I know. She's driving me nuts though." I'd been caught daydreaming at an auction committee meeting and, to avoid admitting my lapse in attention, I'd volunteered to host the auction at the Boathouse, an offer I'd soon regretted.

The preschool was lucky to have the venue though. The Boathouse, located in the beautiful small town of Ericksville, just north of Seattle, was the premier event center in the area. The price they were paying for their Friday night event at a waterfront venue would barely cover a party room for a night at the local Elks Lodge.

I looked at my watch. Almost nine. Without the aid of natural light streaming through a window, time had flown by without me realizing it. I shoved my cell phone and planning notebook into my purse. Anything left on the to-do list could wait until the next day.

"I didn't realize how late it is. Adam is with the kids, but he's probably wondering where I am." I pulled my phone back out of my purse and checked it. Sure enough, two text messages showed up from my husband, asking if I was ok. I fired off a text letting him know I'd be home soon. The text notification beeps hadn't managed to break through my concentration. The auction couldn't come any too soon. I'd been working on it for a very long month already, and I was ready to be done with it.

Beth smiled at me. "It's good for him to have time with the kids." She cocked her head to the side. "Has he said anything else about quitting his job lately?"

Four weeks ago, Adam had announced to me that he planned to quit his job at the Seattle law firm he'd worked at for the last eight years and go into business on his own. I'd been apprehensive about his plan, but hopeful too, because the travel his job required took him away from me and the kids for a couple of weeks out of every month. It hadn't seemed so bad when our son had been born almost four years ago, but after the birth of our daughter seven months ago, I had started to feel overwhelmed with taking care of everything at home by myself.

I stood, grabbing my cell phone off the desk. "No, he's been gone for most of the last few weeks. I need to talk to him and find out what's going on."

"Ok, let me know when you hear something from him. Adam's always been so tight-lipped about everything, ever since he was a little boy." She shook her head. "Sometimes I worry he keeps too much inside."

I walked toward the door, and she moved to allow me to pass. "I'll try to talk to him tonight." I gave her arm a quick squeeze. "I'm going to sit for a few minutes on the deck and can lock up when I'm done. I'll see you tomorrow, ok?"

She nodded, but the concern didn't fade from her face.

I'd been ensconced in the Boathouse's office for the last few hours. When I'd last stepped out to grab a cup of coffee from the kitchen, the sun had still been shining down on Puget Sound. Now, it had started to set over Willowby Island across the water, tinting the sky with a beautiful orange-and-pink glow. This was one of my favorite parts of summer, the breathtaking sunsets.

I pushed open the door to the outer deck and sat on one of the wooden benches to take in the view. The boats on the water had turned their nighttime running lights on, and the windows on the ferry formed a pretty yellow checkerboard.

A breeze blew my hair back, and I lifted my head to take a deep breath through my nostrils. The combination of the rhythmic waves and salt-tinged air never failed to calm me.

I'd recently allowed Beth to talk me into working at the Boathouse as an event planner and marketer because she'd said she wanted to cut back on her workload. I'd known going back to work would be a challenge, but I hadn't expected such long hours right off the bat. Only ten days until the auction. Then it would be back to part-time hours for me at the Boathouse.

My phone vibrated. Adam again.

Are you coming home soon?

Yes, now.

I shoved the phone into my pocket and went back into the Boathouse. I knew Adam was worried, but part of me was irked that it had only been twenty minutes since I'd texted him back and now he was messaging me again. Maybe now he'd understand how I felt when he stayed late at work and didn't call.

I retrieved my purse, then locked the front door and exited to the parking lot. Beth's car was gone, and with the exception of a few people taking a late evening stroll along the sidewalk, the parking lot and surrounding areas were empty. I didn't usually stay this late, and the stillness made me uneasy. My feet crunched on some loose gravel in the parking lot, accentuating the quiet and sending chills down my spine. I was suddenly glad that Adam knew my exact whereabouts.

Chiding myself for being silly, I hurried to my minivan and locked the doors before driving the mile or so up the hill to our house.

Adam must have heard the garage door open because, as soon as I pulled into the garage, he opened the door from the house. Our golden retriever, Goldie, poked his head around Adam's legs, pushing past him to get to me. I closed my car door and rubbed the dog's head. He loyally followed me toward the house.

"Hey," Adam said, stepping back from the door. "I was wondering where you were."

"Trying to slog through the auction stuff, in addition to my regular work at the Boathouse."

"Ah, the auction again. You know, you could always tell Nancy you didn't want to work on it anymore. My mom could probably finish up the prep at the Boathouse, and I'm sure another parent could help out."

I recoiled and stared at him in horror. "You realize if I did that, I'd never hear the end of it, right? Mikey would be shunned at the school."

He raised his eyebrows and laughed. "That bad?"

"Ok, ok, maybe not quite that bad. Seriously, though, Nancy isn't the forgiving type." Nancy had been the lead parent volunteer at my three-year-old's preschool since her oldest child went there, ten years prior. Her youngest child, an immensely spoiled little girl, was in Mikey's class. Her seniority had led to an inflated sense of ownership over the school. Desi and I not so affectionately referred to Nancy and her cronies as the Queen Bees.

I entered the hallway and dumped my purse on a side table. My keys fell out, clattering noisily as they hit the top of the highly polished wood. Pictures of the kids at various stages in their lives hung on the light blue walls near the garage door, ushering me home to family life.

"Have you had dinner yet?" Adam asked.

I halted and sniffed the air. There was the faint smell of

something delicious, but I couldn't make out what it was. "I don't think so?" Coffee and muffins didn't count as dinner, right?

"Well, I made my specialty, chili mac. It's in the fridge. The kids went to bed a few hours ago."

"Dinner sounds good." I walked into the kitchen and pulled the pot out of the refrigerator, setting it on the counter. I grabbed a clean plate out of the dishwasher, piled a mound of chili macaroni and cheese on it, and popped it into the microwave. My eyes roved over the room. Dishes overflowed the confines of the sink, and it looked like Ella and Mikey had thrown food onto the dining room floor. I frowned.

Adam caught me staring at the floor and quickly said, "I'll clean it up. Goldie must have missed a few spots when he gobbled up all of the food the kids dropped at dinner. Sorry, honey, I got the kids in bed, and then something came up at work that I had to take care of. I completely forgot about cleaning the kitchen when I finished."

I poured myself a glass of Chardonnay and sat on a barstool with my food in front of me on the bar-height counter. "It's ok. I'll try to get the sink cleaned out tomorrow." I tasted the cheese and chili concoction. Not bad. It beat the peanut butter sandwich I'd planned to slap together for dinner.

Adam grabbed a paper towel and ran water over it from the sink. "I'll try to help out more when I'm home too." He scrubbed at the hardwood floor until it was free of the yellow and brown food smears.

"Thanks," I said.

"No problem." He grinned at me.

I rubbed my fingers along the smooth edge of one of the

stainless steel forks we'd received as a wedding gift. "You leave tomorrow for Dallas, right?"

He put the used paper towel in the garbage and then turned back to me. "I do. And then I leave a few days later for Atlanta." He sighed. "I'm getting a little tired of this travel. I'd love to be home with you and the kids more often."

This seemed like the right time to bring up his upcoming career change.

"Hey, your mom was asking me when you were going to quit your job." I peered into his eyes. "Have you thought more about it?"

He looked down, suddenly fascinated by his leather shoes. "I've got this project at work that's been dragging on. I owe it to the firm to finish it before I leave. And I still need to find office space in Ericksville and get a business license and do a whole bunch of other things before I can make the jump."

My heart sank. It didn't sound like I'd have a full-time second parent for a long time. When Adam encountered stumbling blocks in a project, they often stalled him for a while. I took a deep breath. "Well, let me know if you need any help with the administrative issues. I'd be happy to help." I swigged the last bit of wine and pushed the glass away from my plate. "If you'd like, I can call Brenda and see if she could show you some potential office spaces to lease." My friend Brenda was a real estate agent in the area, and I knew she'd be happy to help Adam with his office hunt.

He nodded to show he'd heard me, but said nothing.

I stopped with the fork midway from the plate to my mouth and then set it down, pointing to the sink. "Is this going to work?"

"Is what going to work? You working at the Boathouse?"

I nodded. "Yeah."

He came over to the other side of the counter and massaged my shoulders. "It'll be fine. Don't worry. We'll figure everything out."

He sat down next to me, and I turned to face him. "Sometimes I don't think I can handle everything. Your mom has been giving me events to manage, and I've never done this before. I feel like I'm going to mess up." I sighed. "I know once the auction is over, it won't be so bad, but right now I'm up to my eyeballs in stress."

"You are one of the strongest women I know. I think you may have bitten off more than you want to chew right now, but I know you can do it." He brushed a strand of hair away from my face and tucked it behind my ear.

Impulsively, I wrapped my arms around his neck and kissed him. "Thanks. I needed the pep talk."

"No problem." He winked at me. "Anytime. By the way, your mom called me today. She said she'd called you a few times last week, but you never called back."

Rats. I knew I'd forgotten something.

"I meant to call her back but got wrapped up in work stuff. Did she sound mad?"

He shrugged. "No, just concerned."

"It's too late to call her back now, but I'll try to remember tomorrow."

I finished my food and set the plate in the sink on top of all the others. The pots and pans underneath it shifted and creaked ominously. If the stack of dirty dishes made it to the next day without something breaking, it would be a miracle. They needed to be washed, but if I tried to tackle the job while this fatigued, I'd probably break more than if I left them there.

"I'm going to bed now." I yawned. "Is this what it's like to get old?"

"You're thirty-four, not eighty-four." He leaned against the counter.

I yawned again. "Sometimes I feel close to ninety. Maybe it's time I started exercising and eating better." I thought back to the muffin I'd had that day, and the treats Desi made in the Boathouse kitchen for her café. "On second thought, maybe I'll work on just the exercising part first."

He lifted his eyebrows. "*You?* Exercise? I'll believe it when I see it."

"Hey, don't you remember that one time back in college when I ran in a 5k?"

He choked on a sudden eruption of laughter. "You mean the 5k inflatable race where you walked and jogged to one inflatable slide after another? Yeah. That was hardcore." He wrapped his arm around me and pulled me close. "Remember, I was with you. I know you only did it for the chance to jump in a bouncy house like a little kid."

I had to laugh. He was right; that had been my primary motive. I'd never be an athlete, but walking for thirty minutes a day was totally doable. I'd add that to my "after auction to-do" list, which was starting to look almost as intimidating as the "before auction to-do" list.

Adam put his hands on my shoulders to turn me around and pushed me gently toward the stairs. "Now, it's bedtime for you."

I gave in and climbed the stairs. Holding on to the railing, I stopped mid-flight. "Are you coming to bed too?"

"I'll be up soon. I need to take care of something first."

As soon as my head hit the pillow, I conked out. If Adam came to bed sometime during the night, I wasn't aware of it.

2
___

I stumbled downstairs early the next morning, following the scent of brewing coffee. The kids were still asleep in their rooms, and I didn't hear anyone downstairs.

"Adam?" I called out. There was no answer.

Entering the kitchen, I noticed a sticky note on the coffee pot. "I set the timer on the coffee pot for you. I hope you have a wonderful day. I'm off to Dallas. I'll call you when I get in. Love you."

I tossed the note on the counter and poured myself a cup of coffee. When the sleep haze cleared, I realized the sink was scrubbed out and the floor shone from a recent steam mopping. The dining room table had been cleared of crumbs, and even the toaster and refrigerator had been wiped down. He must have been up for hours last night cleaning. I'd never loved my husband more.

After downing two cups of coffee, I woke up the kids and miraculously got them out of the house by a quarter to nine. The Busy Bees preschool started at nine, and I wasn't going to have Mikey be late and give Nancy another reason to be mad at me.

Mikey trudged along behind me as I pushed Ella's stroller down the hill. The day was shaping up nicely, and the weatherman had forecasted temperatures in the mid-seventies. On Puget Sound, boats sailed across the dark blue waters. The ferry to Willowby Island blew its horn to warn away a speed boat that crossed in front of it. What was wrong with those boaters? I certainly wouldn't want to play chicken with a huge car ferry. I stopped for a moment to see if the speed boat would make it to safety, and Mikey crashed into me.

"Mom! Come on, we have to go." He tugged at the hand not holding the stroller.

"Sorry, honey." I cast a glance back at the ferry, which had narrowly averted the smaller boat. Mikey tugged at me again, and I forced myself to stay focused on getting to school on time.

When we were about a block away from the preschool, another mother and son came into view. She was half drag-ging, half carrying him toward the school. Although I couldn't remember seeing him before, the boy was about Mikey's age and obviously didn't want to go to class.

We arrived at the door to Busy Bees at the same time. I held the door open for her, and she deposited her kid in the entry while she signed him in on the computer.

While I waited for the computer, Mikey tried to get past him and the boy lashed out and kicked him in the leg.

"Ow," Mikey cried out. He started to topple over, but I grabbed him by the arm in time to keep him from hitting the ground. The kid who'd kicked him thrashed around on the floor screaming in one of the best temper tantrums I'd ever seen. Tears streamed down his face and into his dark curly hair.

The boy's mother turned around at the sound of Mikey's cry. Her face blanched when she saw him rubbing his leg. "Oh my gosh, did he kick you?"

Mikey stared at her wide-eyed. I nodded and moved Ella safely out of the angry child's reach.

"Daniel! Stop that." The woman turned to me. "I'm so sorry. I'll have a talk with him." She sounded like she was going to break into tears herself. I tried to be calm about it as I'd been that parent before, but I still didn't like having my son hurt. She picked her little boy up and carried him into the classroom, with him screaming the whole way.

"Is he in your class?" I whispered to Mikey.

"Yeah." His eyes were downcast. "Yesterday on the playground, he bit Anthony."

Hmm. Anthony was Mikey's cousin, Desi's son. I'd have to ask her if they'd had other problems with Daniel.

I hugged him. "Sorry, honey. If he does anything to you or your friends, make sure to tell the teacher, ok? He's probably just having a hard time with something, like you were a couple months ago with your dad being gone a lot. Remember?"

He nodded solemnly. "Ok, Mommy. Can I go in now?"

I hugged him again and nudged him gently. "Go."

He ran off toward his classroom.

I signed my son in to school and tried to jet out of there before Nancy could catch me and find something else to change about the auction.

I was wrangling the stroller through the door when she tapped me on the shoulder. I sighed inwardly and turned to face her. Silently, I wished for Ella to start screaming so I could make an excuse to get out of there, but instead, she gave me a look like I was crazy and stuck her thumb in her mouth. *Thanks, kid.*

"Hi, Nancy." I had a lot of work to do, and I prayed this wouldn't take long. Who knew what Nancy would come up with next? I was going to scream if she changed the table linens one more time.

"Jill. I tried to call you yesterday after we met, but you didn't answer the phone." Her white-blonde helmet of hair didn't move as she stared down at me.

I squirmed. There had indeed been several missed calls from Nancy the day before, but unlike those from Adam, I'd ignored them on purpose. For Mikey's sake, though, I needed to make nice with the woman, no matter how much I didn't like her.

I pasted a fake smile on my face. "Sorry about that. I was really busy yesterday evening. What did you need to talk with me about?"

"I'm really busy too," she said snootily. "But I still have time for important things, like my children's school."

I pressed my teeth together so hard they hurt, but it kept me from saying something I'd regret later. I repeated my question. "Well, I'm here now. What did you need?"

"My brother-in-law, Louis Mahoney, has graciously agreed to donate a basket to the auction from his business, Ericksville Espresso. He and my sister-in-law are donating several bags of coffee beans and an espresso machine." A smug smile crept across her lips. "I've been working hard to get donations and make this auction a success."

The implication was that the other parents hadn't been doing anything. My teeth hurt worse. At this rate, I'd need to make a dentist visit soon.

"That's great." I spoke slowly, as though I were talking to one of the preschoolers. "What do you need from me?"

"Someone needs to pick up the donation and store it until the auction." She narrowed her eyes at me. "You do have a storage room at the Boathouse for the auction items, right?"

I wanted to tell her I'd been collecting them and storing them in my bathtub, but I answered truthfully. "Yes. There're quite a few items at the Boathouse already. Can you pick it up since it's coming from your brother-in-law?"

"I can't." She frowned. "My oldest has soccer tonight, and Louis needs it picked up from the warehouse at six o'clock tonight. You'll need to get it. You know where it is, right?"

I took a deep breath. It probably wasn't worth arguing over. Besides, I often passed the Ericksville Espresso warehouse and was curious about what it looked like inside.

"Sure, I know where it is. Does he know I'm coming to pick it up?"

"Yes. But please be there at six because he wants to leave work right after that. He and my sister-in-law have dinner plans."

"I'll be there. Anything else?" I pushed Ella toward the door and awkwardly tried to open it with one hand while using my free hand to thread the stroller through the narrow opening.

"No, that's it for now." She spun around and headed back to the classrooms, not even offering to open the door for me.

That figured. The door tried to squish us several times, but I finally maneuvered the stroller outside. I let the door slam shut behind me and took a deep breath, trying to eradicate the stress I always experienced after dealing with Nancy. The sunlight hit Ella's eyes, and she screamed like a vampire caught in daylight. I leaned over and kissed the baby-soft skin on her forehead, whispering to her, "Now you scream? You couldn't have done that earlier?"

I swear she grinned at me as I flipped the purple flowered stroller cover down to shield her eyes from the sun. My watch read nine twenty. The incident with the angry little boy and the conversation with Nancy had used up all the padding I'd built into my morning schedule. No time for a stop at Elmer's Sea of Fish for an espresso. I'd have to make do with the Boathouse's coffee, which was actually quite good. Beth and my father-in-law, Lincoln, were pretty flexible with my schedule at the Boathouse, but I wanted to get there before nine thirty or I wouldn't have time to finish everything I needed to do before it was time to pick up Mikey. Luckily, my in-laws were happy to have Ella there while I worked.

We headed straight down the hill to the waterfront, passing by the condo project on Sunset Avenue. The burned-out portions of the structure hadn't been rebuilt yet. As happened every time I passed the location, I couldn't help but look up at the empty third floor windows and shudder, remembering my close call with death there. I never wanted to go through anything like that again.

Construction had halted at the project when the owner had died, and I'd heard the new owners were trying to get things up and running in the next few months. For now, the whole lot had been encased by a chain-link fence topped by barbed wire. The overall effect was that of an unfinished prison. Not exactly what we wanted for attracting tourists to downtown Ericksville.

I walked past the ferry dock, Desi's business—the BeansTalk Café—and the lighthouse park area, which took up several blocks. Everything was picture perfect in the June sun. The blue roof of the Boathouse gleamed in front of us, a familiar sight that always made me feel like I was home.

I'd grown up in Idaho but hadn't realized until I moved to Washington how much I hated the claustrophobic feeling of being land-locked. Ericksville was my home now, although I did miss my family back in Couer D'Alene.

A tantalizing fruity scent hit me upon entering the Boathouse. Desi must be busy baking in the kitchen. She used the large commercial kitchen in the Boathouse to prepare pastries for both her café and for the event center. My stomach grumbled noisily at the thought of one of Desi's creations and any idea of a diet went out the door behind me.

Beth heard me come in and met me at the door where I was unbuckling Ella from her seat. "Hi, my sweet girl." She cuddled Desi's seven-week-old daughter in her arms. "Desi's in the kitchen, so I have Lina set up in my office. I'll just bring Ella in there too, and they can both hang out with Grandma today."

I kissed Lina on the head, marveling at how much bigger she'd grown in the last week, although being a preemie, she still fit into some newborn clothes. Then, I set Ella into the Exersaucer my mother-in-law kept in her office.

"Let me know when you want me to come get her." Beth didn't hear me because she was too busy talking to my daughter, who was babbling back at her grandmother in her own language.

I followed the sugary fruit aroma to the kitchen.

Desi was whirling around the room, stirring a pot of a bubbling red substance on the stove and turning on the mixer with the next efficient movement.

"Hey," I said, raising my voice to be heard over the din.

While continuing to stir with one hand, she lifted the

other over her shoulder to say hi to me. With expertise, she flipped the burner knob off and mixer off. She laid the wooden spoon on a spoon rest, removed the pot from the burner, and turned around.

"Good morning," she said cheerily.

"Cherry Danish?" I nodded to the stove and to the pastry dough on the counter. No canned pie filling or pre-made dough for my sister-in-law's baked goods. Her commitment to quality ingredients was a huge reason for the success of her café business.

"Yep." Desi brushed the flour off her hands into the sink, wiped them on a towel, and picked a raisin bran muffin off a cooling rack. She broke it open and took a bite. "Yum. Want one?"

"Sure. I can only talk for a few minutes though. I have to get to work on the auction stuff."

She laughed and put a plated muffin on the counter for me. "Told you."

"I know." I sat on a barstool and slumped over the plate. "I honestly didn't think it would be this bad."

"Well, if you need help, I can pitch in a little. Remember, I worked on it last year, so I have some experience."

"No, you've got too much going on." Desi was only seven weeks postpartum and, with a newborn baby and a booming café business, she had enough to do.

She shrugged. "I can make time. I know dealing with Nancy isn't fun."

"Yeah. In addition to her insane demands, now she's got me running errands for her."

She scrunched her face up. "Like what?"

I took a bite of muffin and swallowed. The bran stuck in the back of my throat. "She wants me to pick up a donation from her brother-in-law." I coughed.

"And she can't get it herself, why?" She brought two cups of coffee to the counter and slid one over to me.

"Apparently she's too busy. I got a lecture about how much she gives to the school and that other parents need to step up." The coffee wasn't that hot, so I swigged some into my mouth to unglue the muffin from my throat.

"Typical." Desi perched on the edge of a stool and removed the tie-dye kerchief that covered most of her hair. Her curly auburn locks sprang free and floated down around her shoulders. She bit into her muffin. "I wonder if she has any clue how much work goes into planning the auction."

"I doubt it. Anyways, her brother-in-law owns Ericksville Espresso—you've seen the warehouse on the east side of town, right? He's got a couple of espresso stands around the area and sells beans to other local businesses.

"I do know of Ericksville Espresso. In fact, I buy the beans for the BeansTalk Café and the Boathouse from them. They have the best flavor profiles of any of the local coffee roasters." She sniffed the steam coming off the hot liquid. "My favorite beans from them have a deep cherry and chocolate flavor. Can you taste it? Isn't it amazing? They also have a dark roast that I offer at the café." She inhaled again before putting her coffee cup down. "Is Louis Mahoney her brother-in-law then?"

"Yeah. I think he's married to Nancy's husband's sister. Or something like that, I didn't dig into it. Have you met him, or do you usually deal with a sales rep?" I sipped my coffee more slowly this time, but I couldn't discern any notes of cherry or chocolate. Desi must have a more sensitive palate than me.

She laughed. "I have met Louis. He hit on me when I was six months pregnant."

"You're kidding." I set my cup down and stared at her.

"Nope. Wish I was." She scowled and shook her head. "He'll hit on any woman. His poor wife."

"I don't understand how some guys think that's ok."

"Me neither." She perked up. "So are you picking the basket up from the warehouse?"

"Yeah, why?"

"Can I come with you? When I met Louis, we were at a coffee bean tasting and I've only ever ordered directly from a sales rep or online. I'd love to see the inside of that place." She rubbed her hands together, and her eyes gleamed. "I bet it's a treasure trove of beans."

I gave her an odd look. Drinking brewed coffee was a big part of my life, but I'd never seen anyone so excited by whole beans.

"I don't know. According to Nancy, I have to be there at six o'clock on the dot." I tapped the counter with my fork for emphasis. "Don't you have the kids tonight?"

Desi's husband, Tomàs, was a police officer with the Ericksville Police Department and often worked night shifts. I'd need to bring my kids with me when I went to pick up the basket, and I didn't think adding another preschooler in a warehouse full of coffee beans sounded like a good idea. A vision of beans cascading down from a bin and scattering across the floor crossed my mind. Ugh. I'd have to really watch Mikey in there. Hopefully it would be a quick in and out, and we could get home in time for me to make something for dinner.

"Oh, didn't Mom ask you?" Desi's face lit up.

"Ask what?" I set the fork down on my empty plate. Beth hadn't said much to me when she'd taken Ella.

"She and Dad want to take the boys and Ella to the Pizza Palace for dinner. They said they'd keep them overnight, and we can pick them up in the morning before they go to work.

My eyes widened. "They want to take all three kids?" Mikey loved the Pizza Palace's arcade and play structure, but the chaotic atmosphere there made me avoid it when at all possible.

She laughed. "Yep, that's what they said. Hey, don't look a gift horse in the mouth. We can leave the kids with them, pick up the auction basket from Ericksville Espresso, and then go down to Alistair's for their Wednesday all-day happy hour. I think we can bring Lina in there as long as we don't sit at the bar. We can pretend we're still carefree single women in our twenties."

I thought about the pile of work sitting on my desk. Without kids distracting me, I could make a huge dent in it.

"I don't know. I've got so much to do."

She stuck her lower lip out at me. "Please? Just think of the yummy polenta fries and flatbread pizzas we can get."

"I'd love to, but I really shouldn't." Her suggestion was tempting though. I did love Alistair's happy hour.

"You need to get out. Your life can't be all about the kids. C'mon. Live a little," she wheedled.

A grin stretched across my face. She was awfully convincing, and it had been a while since we'd had a girls' night. "Oh, all right. I'm in." I picked up our plates and set them in the washing sink behind the counter. "I've got to get to work now if I'm going to play tonight, but I'll meet you here at a quarter to six and we can drive over to the espresso warehouse together."

She hooked the handles of our empty coffee cups on her index fingers and set the mugs next to the plates in the sink. "It's a date."

I checked on Beth and the girls. She filled me in on the

plan to take the kids for pizza and games. I offered to take Ella back with me to my office, but she shooed me away, saying they were having a great time together. I blew kisses to my daughter and Lina, then reluctantly went back to the salt mines.

In my office, I flipped on the light switch and plopped down on my desk chair. I hadn't been working at the Boathouse for very long, and my office reflected that. Other than a calendar from a health insurance company, the walls were blank and boring. I'd need to enlist Mikey to create some colorful artwork to spice up the place. For now, though, I appreciated the austere environment without anything to distract me from my work.

Numerous client files and scraps of notes about the auction stared up at me from my desk. I took a calming breath and dug in, not emerging until lunchtime.

3
____

*A*fter lunch, I dove back into my work, determined to get most of it done so that I could enjoy happy hour with Desi. Somehow, by the end of the day, my desk was almost clear of priority items. Lincoln and Beth had left already with the kids, and there weren't any events scheduled for that evening, so I was alone in the building. They'd locked the door and, when Desi arrived, she pushed the call button, which rang in the offices.

"It's time to party!" she said over the intercom.

"Ha ha. Where's your key?"

"I forgot it at home. Now open the door!"

I buzzed her in. I wouldn't call going out to happy hour partying, but at thirty-four years old with two young kids, that was as close as I was going to get. And, hey, it was a night out without the munchkins.

She appeared at my door with full makeup on, wearing a cute white and pink flowered sundress. Other than the fact that she was carrying Lina in her arms, you'd never know she'd had a baby only the month before. I raised an eyebrow.

"Were we dressing up?" I stared down at my sensible skirt and plain green blouse.

"Oh, you look fine. I'm living it up tonight." Her blue eyes twinkled, and she twirled around, causing the pleats on her skirt to billow out. "It's been a long time since I've gone anywhere fun without a preschooler in tow."

"Ok then." I checked the clock on my computer. Nancy had made it very clear that I needed to pick up the auction donation from her brother-in-law at precisely six o'clock. There wasn't time for me to stop at home to change my clothes. My professional clothes would have to do.

"Are we taking my car or yours?" Desi asked, jangling her keys.

"I'll drive. I'm not sure how big this basket is, so it's probably better to bring my van than your car. You can clip Lina's car seat into the base in our car."

"Good point, your minivan is bigger. Now that I've got two kids, I might need to get one of those myself to lug them and all their gear. Once you get those giant car seats in, there's no room left in the back seat."

I turned off the lights in my office, did a quick check of the other rooms to make sure everything was good to go for the evening, and locked up. Desi's car was the only other vehicle in the lot. A summer breeze came off the water, blowing strands of my long red hair out of the messy bun I'd created atop my head. I removed the hair tie in the car and let my hair fall freely to my shoulders. The older kids were out with their grandparents, Desi and I were on our way to have fun after a brief stop off at Ericksville Espresso, and I wasn't going to let anyone ruin that, not even Nancy.

When we arrived at Ericksville Espresso, it was deserted, except for one champagne-colored Lexus parked in a spot marked 'reserved' near the front door. All of the workers must have gone home already. We exited the car and the stench of roasting coffee beans hit us.

Desi wrinkled her nose and protectively covered a sleeping Lina's head with the cloth covering of her baby carrier. "I love coffee, but I can never get over how gross the beans smell when they're roasting. It would be cool to see the roasting area though."

"No kidding, it's really bad." I'd driven past the building before and smelled the coffee beans, but I'd never encountered it full force. "But I don't think we'll have a chance to tour the facility. We're here to pick up the auction basket, nothing else." I wiggled my eyebrows at her and grinned. "Hey, if you're lucky, maybe you can arrange with Louis for a *private* tour some other day."

Desi smirked and slugged me in the arm. I laughed, then pushed open the door to the office portion of the industrial building. Inside, there was a receptionist's desk with a computer and a counter to greet customers, but it was empty. The air-conditioning blew from an overhead vent, chilling the room and making the distinctive roasting odor less intense.

"Where is everyone?" Desi asked.

"Louis? Mr. Mahoney? It's Jill Andrews," I called out. "I'm here for your donation to the preschool auction." I turned to Desi. "It doesn't look like he's here, but I'm sure Nancy said six o'clock."

She winked at me and put her hand on the door in the rear of the office, which I assumed led to the warehouse. "Well, you did promise to pick up the donation. Maybe it's in here."

I knew what she was up to. "You just want to see the warehouse."

"I want you to fulfill your promise to Nancy," she said

innocently. "If that just happens to mean we get to see the rest of the building, well, that's just icing on the cake."

"Uh huh." I motioned for her to open the door. "You might be right though. What if he's back there in his office and didn't hear us come in? Nancy will never let me hear the end of it if I don't manage to do something so simple as pick up the auction basket." For all that I was teasing Desi about her desire to see the inside of the facility, I wouldn't mind seeing it myself.

I followed her through the door and into a vast warehouse. In the corner was a roasting machine and packaging materials. The room was quiet, so the roaster must not have been running at the moment, although the odor hinted that it had been used recently.

"So cool. I love factory tours." Her gaze was fixed on the roaster.

"Desi, this isn't a tour. We're here for the basket, remember?" I scanned the room for any sign of Louis. I didn't expect to see him in there, but you never knew how involved an owner would be with business operations.

"Yeah, yeah, I know." She wandered over to the assembly line and picked up a package of labels with an image of espresso beans on them and the words, Willowby Dark Roast. "Hey, this is the type of beans I get for the café. I wonder if I could buy some of these one pound bags of beans to sell in the store. Maybe I could even get him to create a new blend for me." She flipped over the back of a bag and read the label. "How does The BeansTalk Blend sound?"

I rolled my eyes at her. "I'm going to try to find Louis. Don't get into any trouble."

She waved her hand in the air at me and strolled over to

the roasting machine, intent on continuing her impromptu tour.

In the far corner of the warehouse were two closed doors, both marked "Office." I strode over to one and knocked on the door. No lights were visible under the door, so I knocked on the other one. A soft glow came through cracks in the doorframe, but no one answered.

I checked over my shoulder. Desi was examining every part of the roasting and packaging operation. I knocked again. Nothing. The door to a small bathroom was ajar, and the light was off. I walked over to the only other door in the warehouse, which was labeled "Break Room." I pushed it open and peeked inside. The light was on and a cup of coffee sat under the mouth of the single-cup coffee maker, but there wasn't anyone there. I touched the ceramic coffee mug. Lukewarm.

Ok, so someone had been here recently. Where was Louis? If Nancy had told me the wrong time after all that, I was going to be mad. I knocked again on the door to the office that had lights on. Nothing. I tried the knob, and it turned easily.

"Mr. Mahoney?" I said as I opened the door. The office was small but expensively furnished with a dark-stained oak desk and a leather desk chair. Abstract art paintings hung on the walls. The overhead light and the computer were on, but I didn't see Louis. Thick rugs covered most of the hardwood floor, in rich contrast to the austere cement floors of the rest of the warehouse. It wasn't how I'd decorate an office, but it gave me ideas for my own.

On the desk was a wicker gift basket, wrapped in plastic. Was that the auction basket? It was smaller than I'd expected, especially if it contained an espresso machine like Nancy had bragged about.

I crossed the room to check it out. Before I reached the side of the desk closest to the basket, I almost tripped on a leg. A man, who I assumed was Louis Mahoney, lay sprawled between an ergonomic desk chair and the desk. I screamed for Desi, then swallowed the lump that had formed in my throat and forced myself to move closer to him. His arms were outstretched, as if grabbing for something, and the middle drawer to the desk was open. Paper clips, some hard candy, and a few rubber bands were strewn across the floor next to the man.

His face was shadowed by the desk, and I knelt on the rug to see it closer up. His lips were purple and puffy, and his eyelids were swollen so badly that I couldn't see his eyes. There was no way he was alive. Just in case, I felt for a pulse, but his skin was cool and his heartbeat nonexistent.

"What's going on?" Desi asked as she burst through the door. "I was going to smell some of the other beans. This place is awesome! They should totally offer public tours."

I grabbed her wrist and drug her over to the desk, pointing at the body on the floor. "That is what's going on."

The color drained from her face. "Oh my gosh. Is that Louis Mahoney?" She handed me Lina and dropped down to him to check for a pulse too. "It is. And he's dead," she said in a hollow voice.

"I know." To me, my voice sounded far-off, like it was coming out of someone else's mouth.

"What do we do?" She looked very unlike her usual take-charge self.

I handed Lina back to her and pulled out my phone.

"I'll call for help." With trembling fingers, I called 911. They said they'd send an ambulance and to stay with him.

"Do you think he had a heart attack?" Desi inched backward toward the door, her eyes glued to the body. I joined her.

"I don't know." We hovered silently in the doorway, alternating between staring at each other and the body.

The basket on the desk caught my eye again. I knew I should respect the dead and stay away from the body, but curiosity got the best of me.

"Do you think that's the auction donation?" I whispered to Desi. After stumbling on Louis's body, I'd completely forgotten the reason I'd come over near his desk in the first place.

"I don't know, but you can't take it now." She didn't move from the doorway.

I ignored her and tiptoed closer to the basket. It wasn't full of coffee products as Nancy had promised. The plastic encasing the wicker basket had been unwrapped and lay in folds beneath the basket. I nudged the basket to turn it slightly, the plastic crackling as it moved. It still contained a bottle of chocolate wine. Chocolate truffles were scattered across the desk. A fancy violet ribbon with "Watkins Real Estate" stretched across the basket like a sash on a beauty pageant queen. An ornate bow in a slightly different shade of purple lay on the desk next to it. I sucked in my breath.

"Desi," I hissed. "It's not the auction basket—it's from Brenda."

"Brenda?" she asked. "As in our Brenda? Sara and Dara's mom? Why would there be a basket from her here?"

"Yes, Brenda from the preschool." Our friend Brenda Watkins owned a successful real estate firm in Ericksville. "It looks like something she'd give a client."

Desi approached the desk. She pointed at something next to the basket. "That doesn't look like something you'd say to a business associate."

I followed her gaze to a piece of thick card stock. Someone had written on it with loopy cursive penmanship.

Louis—I'm looking forward to seeing you Friday night and sharing the bottle of wine. I know it's your favorite. I'll see you at my place at seven. Kisses, Brenda.

Acid churned in my stomach. I turned to Desi, my eyes wide. "Wait, what? Do you think she was dating him?" I'd known her for two years, and Brenda had never seemed the type to go out with a married man. Her ex-husband was now her ex because he'd cheated on her. She had no tolerance for cheaters.

Desi shrugged. "I don't know, but something was going on between her and Louis, and I don't think it was a simple business transaction."

"Should we hide the note? What if his wife sees it?" I reached out to touch the note, and she swatted my hand away.

"Don't."

"Why not? Would you want to find something like this in your husband's office?"

"Tomàs would never cheat on me." She glanced at the note. "But he also would never forgive me if I messed with the scene of someone's death."

I sighed. "Ok, but I hate to see Brenda involved with this. Now everyone will see the card and think badly of her. I'm sure there's a logical reason for her to have sent him the basket."

"Probably." Desi didn't look too certain.

The whole situation seemed surreal and, as we contemplated the meaning of the basket, we almost forget that hidden on the other side of the desk was a dead man.

Voices floated into the office. We'd been so isolated in the back of the warehouse that I hadn't heard the ambulance approach the building or the emergency personnel enter.

"We're back here," I called out.

Two EMTs burst into the room and checked the man's pulse. Desi and I left the room to allow them to do their thing. "He's gone," one of the EMTs said loudly to his partner as we exited.

"What do we do now?" Desi whispered to me. The roasting coffee smell was making me dizzy. I didn't know how anyone could stand to be in there for very long. "Are we allowed to leave?"

"I don't know. When I found Mr. Westen's body, the police came right away."

"Well, good thing you have experience in this. This is nerve-wracking."

I glared at her. It wasn't exactly something I wanted to have experience in.

Lina whimpered and stirred in her front pack. As if on cue, the police showed up. Desi and I answered all of their questions and were finally allowed to leave after an hour, probably because the police didn't want to hear Lina's cries anymore.

When we were safely in my minivan in the parking lot and out of earshot of the emergency personnel, we started talking over each other.

"Do you think he had a heart attack?" she asked.

"Do you think he was murdered?" I asked at the same time.

We stared at each other.

"Sheesh. This is crazy." Desi gazed out the window and then back at me. "Why would you think he was murdered?"

"I don't know. The police were asking a lot of questions."

I shot a glance at the building. "Nancy is going to kill me for not getting that auction donation."

"I think you have an excuse," she said. "Besides, she'll be too busy mourning him to worry about the basket."

"I guess." I stared back at the building. Red and blue lights flashed atop the two police cars and an aide car in the parking lot. The door to the lobby had been propped open to allow access. As I watched, a third police car pulled up. I turned around to view the middle seats in my van. Even Lina's eyes were fixed on the happenings outside.

"Do you think Tomàs is here?" I asked.

"I don't know. Maybe we should get out of here before he finds out I was involved with this. He tends to get a little overprotective when he thinks I'm in danger."

"He loves you. And you know he's going to find out anyway."

"Yeah, I know, but maybe I can keep him from finding out for a few hours. Hey, I'm starving. Do you still want to get something to eat?" She pulled her phone to check a website. "The Alistair's menu says they serve food until ten, so we still have time."

My mouth dropped open. "How can you eat after that?"

"I can always eat." She shrugged. "I'm a nursing mother. I've got to get those extra calories in."

I didn't feel that hungry after visiting Ericksville Espresso, but I figured going out to eat would be a better distraction than sitting at home alone, reliving the memory of seeing Louis's body. "Yeah, let's go."

As we were driving away from the warehouse, a black BMW roared past us. Desi pulled over to the side of the road, and we watched in the rearview mirror as the car pulled up to Ericksville Espresso and a woman with blonde hair jumped out and ran over to the police officers.

"Do you think that's his wife?" Desi's eyes were glued to the mirror.

I craned my head around, trying to get a better look. "I don't know. Nancy said that I had to be here at six because he was going out to dinner with his wife, so maybe he didn't come home and she grew worried." I shrugged. "I'd probably do that if Adam didn't come home if we had plans and I couldn't reach him on the phone."

"I guess." She tore herself away from the mirror and turned to me, chewing on her lower lip. "I do feel a little guilty about leaving the note like that. If that's his wife, she's probably going to see it, just as we left it."

"Yeah." I was quiet for a moment. "You were right though. We couldn't touch it. Not if this wasn't a natural death."

She shivered. "I really hope you're totally off base with thinking he could have been murdered. With the exception of Mr. Westen, that kind of thing just doesn't happen in our little town."

"Ericksville may be a small town, but bad things can happen anywhere." I turned back around. "Can we get out of here? I'd like to try to forget this ever happened, ok?"

"Me too." Desi put the car in drive and maneuvered back onto the street.

4

To my relief, Nancy wasn't at the preschool when I brought Mikey there the next morning. I wasn't positive she'd think finding Louis's body was an excuse for not getting the basket, and I didn't want to talk to her about the basket or her brother-in-law. To tell the truth, the woman scared me a little.

At two o'clock, I walked the few blocks over to the BeansTalk carrying Ella in her front pack. The temperature was in the low seventies—not too hot, but pleasant with the breeze coming off the water. People strolled the paved pathways around the lighthouse, and a bicyclist rode past me.

"Hey," Desi greeted me when I walked through the door. "Coffee?" She held up a mug.

I nodded. "Yes, please." I perused the bakery case and selected a double-baked almond croissant.

She rang up my order, put the croissant on a plate, then scanned the café. "I think it's time for my break too."

I looked around. "Where's Lina?" Desi usually took her infant daughter to work with her.

"Tomàs has the day off, so he's got her for the afternoon." She plucked a blueberry muffin from the case and brought it and her coffee over to a table. Immediately, she took a huge bite, inhaling her food so fast that if I hadn't eaten dinner with her the night before, I'd worry she hadn't eaten for days. "It's been so busy this morning that I didn't have a chance to eat breakfast or lunch."

I joined her at the table and used the front pack to prop Ella up in a high chair. She babbled at me and reached for my food. I set a few pastry crumbs in front of her, and she picked them up, rolling them between her fingers. "I can't get my mind off finding Louis's body."

"I know." She put her muffin on the plate, and the corners of her mouth turned down. "I tried to get information from Tomàs about it, but he said they don't know anything yet."

"He probably had a heart attack." I said it to reassure her, but his eyes and lips had been horribly swollen, so I wasn't sure of that.

"So what do you think about the gift basket from Brenda? Do you think she knew he was married?"

I shook my head. "I doubt it. Her ex-husband cheated on her. I can't imagine she'd ever be 'the other woman.'"

"Good point." Desi sipped her coffee, which was heavily laced with cream.

I sighed, then glanced at the clock. "Preschool is almost over. Do you want me to pick up Anthony? We walked today, so I can get him and bring him to the café for you. That way you don't have to leave."

"That would be great, thanks." She beamed at me.

I was finishing the last few crumbs of my croissant when my phone rang. With sticky fingers, I gingerly plucked it from my bag and checked the caller ID. "It's Brenda," I hissed to Desi.

Her eyes widened. "Are you going to ask her about Louis?"

I shook my head and answered the phone. "Hey."

"Jill?" Brenda's voice quivered, instantly setting me on edge.

"What's wrong?"

Desi shot me a "'what's going on'" look.

"Would you be able to pick up my girls and take them home with you?"

"Sure," I said slowly. "Why?" Although we'd been friends for a while, she'd never asked me to do that before.

"I'm not going to be able to get there in time. Can you please do it?"

"Of course." I hesitated. "Is something wrong?" A vision of Brenda being held hostage flitted across my mind, and I pushed it away. "Are you ok?"

"Yeah." The sounds of other people in the room with her echoed through the phone.

"I'll take them home with me—just let me know when you want to pick them up. The girls are welcome to stay as long as you'd like."

"Thanks, Jill. I appreciate it." She disconnected.

I couldn't take my eyes off the phone even after she'd hung up. Something was very wrong.

Desi stared at me. "What was that about?"

"I don't know. Brenda wants me to pick up the girls from school and take them home with me."

"Maybe she got hung up at a real estate showing or something."

"I don't think so. I got the feeling she was worried about something." I picked at my paper napkin.

Desi picked up our plates and cups, and carried them

behind the counter. "I'm sure she's ok. Maybe she heard about Louis's death and is upset about it?"

"Maybe." My brain spun with worry about Brenda, and I wanted to call her back and press her for the truth, but I had to get moving or I wouldn't get to the preschool in time for pickup.

I pushed my chair back and stood. Desi picked Ella up from the high chair and snuggled her while I wriggled into the front pack. Ella pulled at her aunt's hair, and Desi laughed while disentangling the baby's fingers. She held her out to me, and I situated her on my chest, where she immediately focused on trying to yank my hair.

"Are you sure you can manage walking back here by yourself with all four of the preschool kids?"

"I'll be fine," I said with more confidence than I felt. I pushed the door open, causing the bells over it to chime. "I'll see you in a bit with Anthony."

She smiled. "Thanks, Jill."

I walked past the ferry landing and Elmer's Sea of Fish. The ferry was at the dock, and I had to wait a few minutes to cross with all the traffic coming off the boat. I climbed the few blocks uphill toward the preschool, marveling at how heavy Ella had become in the last few months. It wouldn't be much longer that I could comfortably carry her in the front pack.

I quickly walked past the tall chain-link fences guarding the condos, not wanting to think of the last place I'd seen someone dead. At Busy Bees, I paused in front of the door, taking a deep, calming breath. I'd gone from picking up my one kid to taking three extra kids on our walk home. In addition to that, I really didn't want to deal with Nancy today and having four kids to wrangle instead of one would make it much more likely I'd run into her.

Parents were already signing out their kids when I went inside. I said hi to a few of them that I knew from the auction committee.

"Hey," Lindsay Lee said. "I procured a huge gift basket from the sporting goods store. Is it all right if I drop it off at the Boathouse?" Her hair was wrapped up in a neat bun, and she wore a bright turquoise shell under a black blazer. On her feet were spiky designer high heeled shoes. I felt like a slob in comparison, although I'd been at work earlier and was wearing a nice gray skirt and navy blouse. With shoes like hers, there was no way I could have made the trek around town with the kids.

I nodded. "I'll be there tomorrow morning, but if you want to drop it off earlier, just ask for Beth or Lincoln and they can show you where to store it."

"Thanks!" She flashed me a smile, revealing pearly white teeth, grabbed her child's hand, and breezed out the door.

I made my way into the three-year-olds classroom and found Mikey and Anthony playing Legos together on the colorful alphabet rug.

"C'mon, boys. Time to go."

"Do we have to?" Mikey pleaded.

Anthony stared at their Lego castle with disappointment. "Yeah, Aunt Jill. Do we have to leave? We've been working hard on this."

Their teacher, Ms. Shana, swooped in, beaming at the boys. "Wow, you have been working hard on it. I love it!" She knelt in front of them and gestured at an empty white bookcase. "How about I put the castle up on the shelf over there? Then you can play with it tomorrow afternoon, ok?"

Mikey cast a glance at the shelf. He pursed his lips and opened his mouth as if about to complain.

I grabbed his hand. "That sounds like a great idea."

He shut his mouth and relented. "Let's go, Anthony."

I helped Ms. Shana carry their creation over to the shelf.

"There you are." Nancy entered the room, followed by Brenda's girls. "Brenda called and said you were going to get the girls."

She turned to the girls. "Go get your backpacks. You're going to go home with Mikey's mom today."

They looked up at her. "Where's Mommy?" one of them asked.

"She got stuck at work and asked me to get you guys. You'll have a play date with Mikey this afternoon, ok?" I had no idea what was going on with Brenda, but I wasn't going to tell her kids that. They scurried off to get their backpacks from their cubbies in the other room.

Nancy huffed. "That figures. Brenda can't even be bothered to pick up her own kids. Probably off wrecking some other home." She looked at me defiantly.

I stepped back. Whoa. Apparently she knew about Brenda and Louis. She didn't seem that broken up about her brother-in-law's death, but was oddly concerned about him committing adultery.

I gestured for the boys to pick up their backpacks, which lay on the floor next to the Legos. I glared at Nancy. "I'm not sure what you're talking about. Brenda is a great mom, but I'll be sure to pass on your sentiments to her."

Her nasty expression wavered. Apparently the bully wasn't so confident about talking behind someone's back when it would get back to her victim. She pursed her lips and spun on her heels, rushing out of the room.

Something whirred behind me, and I turned around to see the gerbils in their cage, running side by side on a pair of wheels. They seemed to be enjoying the gerbil playground we'd bought for them. Mikey came up next to me.

"Now can we take them home, Mommy?"

I stared at him like he'd grown wings. "Honey, we can't take them home with us because we already have Goldie and Fluffy." I congratulated myself on the perfect excuse. Our dog and cat were a convenient reason to not take the gerbils home, but the truth was, I hated rodents and the class pets were never coming home with us. Even though they'd once saved my life, I had to draw the line somewhere.

"But everyone else gets to take them home for the weekend," Mikey whined.

Brenda's girls came back in with their backpacks and slowly approached me. "Are we really going home with you?" one of them asked.

"Yes, honey." I patted her blonde head, grateful for the distraction. "Now, you girls look so much alike that I'm not sure who I'm talking to."

"I'm Sara," said the girl in front of me. "That's my sister, Dara."

"Well, I'm excited you're coming home with us, and so is Mikey. Right, Mikey?" I eyed him.

"Yeah," he grumbled. "Can Anthony come over too?"

Just what I wanted—four preschoolers and a baby at my house. My furniture would never be the same again. "Uh, I think his mom misses him. We'll take him to the café first."

I whispered to the kids, "Maybe Anthony's mom will have cookies for you when we drop him off."

"Cookies?" Dara asked, with a gleam in her eyes.

"Yeah!" Anthony made a beeline for the door as I signed them all out. "My mom makes the best cookies. Let's go!"

I tried to hold on to as many hands as I could, but unfortunately, I wasn't an octopus. "All right, everyone grab the hand of a buddy and follow me." I walked out the door and herded them onto the sidewalk. "We'll drop Anthony off at his parents' café, down by the ferry." The girls nodded and held hands while skipping along the sidewalk. Mikey stopped to examine something along the side of the road, attracting his cousin.

"Is that a dead slug?" Anthony asked.

"I think so," Mikey said gleefully.

The girls stopped and made disgusted faces. "Eww," they said in unison.

I put my hands on the boys' shoulders and led them back over to the girls. "Focus, boys."

We finally made it the few blocks to the café, the kids getting more and more excited about getting a treat the closer we got to the café.

"I hope Anthony's mom has chocolate chip cookies. I love chocolate chip," Dara said.

"I told Mommy I wanted chocolate chip cookies yesterday, but she made peanut butter cookies instead," her sister complained.

"Yeah. They were gross."

They pressed their noses into the glass door of the BeansTalk Café, and I had to thread my hand through their eager hands to push on the door handle. They burst into the room in a torrent of high-pitched voices.

Desi looked up from her perch behind the counter, as did the other patrons. She jumped off the chair and came over to us.

"I may have promised them all cookies," I said, only feeling slightly guilty about it.

She raised her eyebrows and grinned. "Ok, kids, what kind of cookies do you want?"

"Chocolate chip!" they answered with resounding enthusiasm.

With a pair of metal tongs, Desi bagged cookies individually and handed one to each child.

"Thanks, Anthony's mom," Sara said, her mouth already streaked with melted chocolate.

"Yummy," Dara said.

Mikey hugged Desi. "Yeah, thanks."

"Have fun," Desi said as I led the other kids to the door.

I shot her a pained look. "Thanks."

With one less kid, it was slightly easier to walk through town, but by the time we arrived at our house, I was beat. I had no clue how the preschool teachers managed to make it through a day with twenty kids without having a nervous breakdown.

5

When I opened the door to our house, Goldie tried to push past me, and Dara screamed when she saw him. I quickly shut the door.

"Don't worry, he won't hurt you," I said.

She cowered behind Mikey and Sara, and didn't respond.

"A dog growled at her one time, and now she's scared of them," Sara explained.

"Ok, I'll lock him up. Wait here and don't move." They nodded. I grabbed Goldie's collar and led him into Adam's study.

I opened the door and, miraculously, all the kids were exactly where I left them. Dara peered around the door, as if suspicious that Goldie was going to lunge at her from behind the couch.

"He's locked up in a room back there." I pointed down the hall. Dara nodded and smiled faintly. "Mikey, why don't you get some of your toys out for the girls to play with?"

He shot me a withering look but disappeared upstairs

for a few minutes and returned with some Fisher-Price Little People toys.

After I had an hour to wind down at home, I got the kids a healthier snack of peanut butter and apple slices. Brenda still hadn't called, and I was getting more worried as the afternoon dragged on. Mikey had begrudgingly shared his Legos with the girls, and they had all been playing nicely. Ella had fallen asleep in her crib, and the house was almost quiet as the kids ate their snack. I leaned back to relax on our comfy couch. Of course, right then, my cell phone buzzed on the coffee table in front of me. I lunged for it, thinking it was Brenda.

"Has Brenda come for the girls yet?" Desi asked without even a hello first.

I swung my legs back up on the couch and glanced at the kids sitting on the kitchen stools. Mikey was entertaining his guests by holding apple slices up in front of his eyes and smiling menacingly at them. Both girls laughed at his antics and imitated him.

"No, I haven't heard anything yet." I closed my eyes for a moment and took a deep breath. "Nancy knows about the gift basket that Brenda gave Louis."

She gasped. "Already?"

"Apparently." I sighed. "I knew we should have taken the note."

"You know we couldn't do that, right?"

"I know, but when I picked the kids up, she made some nasty remark about Brenda being a home-wrecker."

"Sheesh. In front of the kids?"

"The girls were in another room at the time, and the boys were playing Legos, oblivious to anything going on around them."

My phone beeped, alerting me to an incoming phone

call. I held the phone away from my ear to see who was calling.

"Desi, I've got to go. Brenda's calling."

"Ok. Let me know what you find out from her."

"I will." I clicked over to Brenda.

"Jill?" Her voice sounded a little stronger than it had earlier.

"Yes. Hi."

"Thanks for getting the girls. Brad is out of town, or I would have asked him to get them."

"No problem." I knew I was lucky to have my in-laws around to babysit for me. Not everyone was that fortunate. I didn't want to ask her when she was coming to get her kids.

"I'm done here." She sighed. "I'll see you in a few minutes."

"See you then."

I turned to the girls. "Dara, Sara—your mom will be here in a few minutes."

"Yay!" they said.

Disappointment crossed Mikey's face. "I wanted to show them my Jake and the Never Land Pirates tree house."

"You probably have time. Why don't you show it to them now, before their mom gets here?"

The kids all ran off upstairs.

Brenda rang the doorbell a few minutes later, and I let her in. She wore a black sheath dress with a trendy matching silver bracelet and necklace set. On her feet were heels that were probably designer made. Although her overall appearance was put together, her makeup couldn't hide the fact that she'd been crying, and I could see the tenseness in her neck. She glanced around the living room. "Where are the girls?"

I pointed to the ceiling. "Mikey wanted to show them

something in his bedroom upstairs. Can I get you a cup of coffee? He has enough toys up there that it could be a while."

Her mouth twitched. "I should probably get going." She looked longingly at the kitchen. "But I guess it wouldn't hurt to stay for a cup."

I pulled two mugs down from the cupboard and set them on the counter next to the coffee pot, while she sat down on a barstool. "Do you want room for cream?"

"No, I'm trying to cut back."

I nodded and filled both of them almost to the brim with the freshly brewed coffee I'd made when I got home.

"Here you go." I set the mug in front of her on the bar and perched on a stool across from her. "So what's going on? Are you ok?"

She stared into her cup.

"Not that I mind getting the girls from school, but you sounded odd when I spoke with you earlier."

Her eyes filled with tears, and she swiped them with the back of her hand. "This is going to sound awful, but the police were at my house, questioning me."

"About Louis Mahoney's death?"

Her head bobbed up sharply. "Yes, how did you know?"

I tapped my fingers on the edge of my coffee cup. "Desi and I found his body last night." I glanced down and then up to meet her eyes. "We saw the gift basket you sent him and the note you wrote to him."

Her face crumpled, and the tears fell faster. "I didn't know he was married, I swear."

I handed her a tissue and although she dabbed furiously at her face, her mascara had begun to run.

"We figured as much. But why were the police questioning you?"

She took a big breath. "They said Louis was murdered, and now I'm a suspect."

Shoot. I knew we should have taken that note.

"Murdered?" I echoed. My heart beat faster. I'd been through a murder investigation with Mr. Westen's death a few months ago and had really hoped Louis had died of natural causes.

"What happened to him?" I hadn't seen any noticeable evidence of foul play when we'd found his body.

"They said he died of anaphylactic shock," she said in a weak voice.

"As in he was allergic to something? Like a bee sting?" The window hadn't been open while we were there, although I supposed it was possible for there to have been a bee in his office.

"Apparently he was extremely allergic to peanuts." She pushed her coffee mug away and propped her head in her hands, her fingers tapping against her forehead.

"So what makes the police think he was murdered? Couldn't he have accidentally eaten something with peanuts in it?"

"Because it was the chocolates I gave him that killed him."

"You knew he had a peanut allergy, and you gave him those anyways?"

"No!" she said sharply, then looked guiltily at the stairs as if checking to make sure her outburst hadn't been over-heard by the kids. In a softer voice, she explained. "The chocolates had no peanuts in them ... at least not naturally. Someone injected them with some sort of peanut product."

I twisted my thumbs together and met her eyes. "And you knew nothing about it?"

47

"Jill!" she admonished. "Seriously? I had nothing to do with it. I really liked him."

"Ok, sorry. I wasn't thinking. But this is such a mess. How did you get involved with him anyway?"

Something thumped loudly upstairs. We both gazed at the ceiling, but there were no cries of pain following the noise, so we relaxed. Mikey had probably knocked a toy off the bookshelf onto the floor.

She sighed. "Louis and I met when he contacted me about leasing additional warehouse space. I showed him a few places, and we got to talking. You probably wouldn't guess it if you met him briefly, but he could be really sweet." She stared into my eyes. "You have to believe me. I had no idea he was married. I'd never have gone out with him if I'd known."

She'd never given me any reason to doubt her integrity. "I do believe you. But how did the peanuts get into the chocolates?"

"I have no idea. Someone must have put it in the chocolates after I dropped off the basket." She glanced at the stairs again and lowered her voice. "This can't be happening now. This is the worst possible time. Brad and I have always shared custody in the past, but he's talking about moving out-of-state, and he wants to take the girls with him. If the courts find out I'm suspected of murder, they'll never let me keep them."

This kept getting worse and worse. "Maybe the police will figure out who really killed him soon."

"I don't know. They seemed pretty convinced it was me. Said I must have known he'd lied to me about not being married, and I killed him for it." She made a sound, a harsh rendition of her normal laugh.

"Mommy?" A little girl's voice interrupted us. Brenda

wiped her eyes with the tissue and spun around to face her daughter. She slid off the stool.

"Hey, sweetie." She hugged Dara. Sara came down the stairs and joined their hug.

"Can we go home now?" Sara asked.

"Yep. I'm making macaroni and cheese for dinner. Does that sound good to you?" They gave each other high fives and grinned at her.

"Can you please go get your backpacks?" When the girls were out of earshot, she said to me in a wavering voice, "I can't lose them. They're my everything."

I nodded. I wanted to help my friend, but I didn't know how. "I can see if Desi's husband Tomàs knows anything about the case."

"Would you?" Hope tinged her tone.

"Of course. I'll call Desi tonight and ask her to find out. She can usually wheedle some information out of him. And I'll see if I can find anything else out." I wrapped my arms around her. "Don't worry, everything will work out."

"I hope so." The girls came back into the room, and she walked to the door with them. Before leaving, Brenda turned to me. "Thanks for everything, Jill."

I smiled at her. "No problem. That's what friends are for." I shut the door behind them and leaned against it. Asking Tomàs about the murder was a good start, but if I really wanted to help my friend, I needed to do a little snooping. Anything I could find out about Louis would help, and I knew where to start.

$\mathcal{U}$nfortunately, auction business took priority over snooping around Louis's murder, and I had to practically chain myself to my desk Friday morning to make sure I was on track with the auction.

Beth poked her head into my office. "Hey, just thought I'd check in on you. How's the auction planning going?"

"Going good. I think we've finally got the menu nailed down and have the attendee count finalized, at least until Nancy changes her mind again."

"Great." She scanned my desk and then my face, as if trying to determine how to proceed.

"What's up?" I pushed my chair back and stretched my arms over my head.

"I know you're busy, but we have a last-minute wedding, and I'd like you to take care of it. Do you think you have time for it with your other commitments?"

I dropped my hands to my sides and stared at her. I was supposed to be part-time at the Boathouse, and I had an almost full-time workload. If it had been anyone else, I would have said something, but with Beth being my mother-in-law, I had to tread carefully. She seemed to sense my concern.

"It's nothing major," she said hastily. "It's a small, midweek wedding. Probably about forty people."

I relaxed slightly. That didn't sound too bad. "When is it?" With a few weeks to plan, I could easily pull that off.

She blushed. "Next Tuesday."

"As in four days from now? You're kidding me, right?" I looked at my calendar. It was already Friday, and the auction was only a week away. I'd also been working on a wedding and a graduation party for the coming weekend.

"No." She sighed. "They decided to get married as soon as possible because the groom is shipping out with the Navy in two weeks. The bride didn't want to give up her chance at a formal wedding, so they asked if we could squeeze them in. Tuesday was the only day that we had open that worked with their schedules. I'd do it, but I have a doctor's appointment on Tuesday afternoon that I can't reschedule, and I'd like for someone to be here that day in case we need to tweak anything with the event."

My heart softened. Planning a wedding on such short notice would be stressful, but I knew what it was like to be separated by distance from my spouse. If this made their lives any easier, I couldn't say no.

Beth's words sunk in, and I looked up from my calendar and scrutinized her face. "Is your doctor's appointment anything I should be concerned about?" A few months ago, I'd discovered Beth had a heart condition. I hoped her health hadn't deteriorated.

"Nope." She waved her hand dismissively. "Just a check-up." She glanced at Ella lying in the corner on her mat. The baby lifted herself up from her tummy and giggled for her grandma.

A smile crossed my lips. Ella was growing so fast and would soon be up and walking. I'd brought her to work with me so far, but in another few months, I'd need to figure out a more permanent childcare solution for the times when Beth or I were unavailable.

Beth scooped her up and kissed her forehead. "Do you mind if I take her for a while?"

I laughed. "Go right ahead. Actually, I was going to ask you if you'd mind watching her for an hour or two. I'm going to head over to Ericksville Espresso and see if I can still get the gift basket they promised for the auction."

She raised her eyebrows. "Weren't you and Desi just there when you found Louis Mahoney's body?"

"Yes, but the reason we were there in the first place was to get the gift basket." I shuffled some paperwork around on my desk. "After the police arrived, we didn't think it prudent to ask about the whereabouts of the basket for the auction. But it's something Nancy had arranged—Louis Mahoney was her brother-in-law—and I don't want to find out what will happen if an auction item she procured doesn't show up at the auction."

"I'm sure she'd understand, right?" Beth struggled to keep a straight face. She'd heard too many horror stories about Nancy Davenport over the last two years from Desi and me.

I scrunched up my face in answer, and she laughed.

"I'll take Ella. Go, get the basket. I don't want anything bad to happen to you if it doesn't show up. I'll put the information about the wedding on your desk, and I'll let the clients know you'll call them about it in a few hours."

"Thanks, Beth." I pulled the bottom desk drawer out and retrieved my purse. Slinging it over my shoulder, I stood and walked to the door. She followed me out, carrying my daughter.

"Say bye-bye to Mommy." She waved Ella's hand at me. I blew a kiss at the baby, who blew bubbles back at me. I left the Boathouse grateful that I'd been given the opportunity to work there. The stress could get to me sometimes, but there weren't many other places that I would find fulfilling work and still be able to maintain some semblance of a work-life balance. And having a built-in babysitter didn't hurt.

I drove up to Ericksville Espresso and maneuvered into a parking space. Last time I'd seen this parking lot, it was full of emergency vehicles and illuminated by flashing lights. Now it had returned to the utilitarian warehouse that I'd entered two days ago. A red sports car was parked near the front door, but the reserved parking spot was conspicuously empty.

I pushed the swinging door open to the main reception area, still surprised at how normal everything looked. Like before, the desk was empty, but I heard people talking just beyond the door to the warehouse. While I waited for the receptionist to come back, I perused the pictures on the walls. Someone had hung photographs of coffee beans on the walls. Every picture depicted a different style of roasted coffee bean, some a dark, burnt color and others more of a medium brown. Desi would be fascinated with the color variations. When we'd been in here before, neither of us had given the front office a second thought after we went into the warehouse.

The door slammed open, causing the roasting coffee

odor to invade the room. A woman in her early thirties strutted into the office, teetering on impossibly high heels. She wore a tight red tank top and had more makeup plastered on her tanned skin than I wore in a year. She glanced at me with annoyance, then sat down behind the desk without saying anything to me.

A sign on the desk read "Terri Scalia." I approached the counter and cleared my throat, hoping to get her attention. She ignored me.

"Excuse me, Terri?"

At the sound of her name, she finally deigned to notice me. "Can I help you?"

I cringed. Her nasal voice grated on me like fingernails on a chalkboard. "Yes, I'm Jill Andrews. I'm here to pick up the basket for the Busy Bees Preschool Auction."

She shot me a look like I was crazy and sniffed in the air. "An auction basket?" Her eyes narrowed. "You aren't talking about that tiny wicker basket of chocolates that the real estate woman sent for Louis, are you?"

My heart pounded, and my chest felt like someone was sitting on it. She'd seen Brenda's basket. The question was; was it before or after the chocolates were tampered with?

"I don't think so, but maybe?" I lied. "What was in that basket?"

"It was the chocolates that killed Louis." She glared at me as if I had something to do with his death. "I think there was something else in there, but I didn't unwrap the basket."

"So it was wrapped in plastic when you received it?"

"Yeah, I put it on my boss's desk before I left for lunch that day. Why are you so concerned about it? Is it the basket you were looking for, or not?"

"I don't think so. I'm pretty sure the basket the preschool

was promised contained coffee products from Ericksville Espresso."

She narrowed her eyes. "Then why are you asking me questions about it? Are you working with the police or something?"

"No, no, nothing like that," I said quickly. If Tomàs found out I was snooping, I'd never hear the end of the safety lectures. "Brenda, the real estate agent who sent the basket with the chocolates, is actually a friend of mine."

"You're friends with *her*?" Animosity rang from her voice.

"Yeah, why? Do you know her? Had she come in here before?"

"The only time I ever saw her was when she dropped off the gift basket, but I know of her. Well, I knew he'd been sneaking around with some woman." She laughed harshly. "Louis's wife, Sandy, was furious when she found out after his death that he was having an affair with her. She came storming in here this morning, asking me if I knew anything about it."

It wasn't my place to talk about Brenda's relationship with Terri's boss, but I wanted to defend my friend. "I don't think she knew he was married."

"Right, and I'm Santa Claus," she scoffed. "Well, she wasn't the first of his affairs."

Poor Brenda. Although she'd said he was sweet, the guy sounded like a real jerk. Terri didn't know anything about the auction basket, and I wanted to get back to work, but she seemed like she wanted to talk now, so I played along.

"Really?" I asked conspiratorially. "Did his wife know about the other affairs?"

Her face pinked up.

"No, she never knew." She stopped, as if just now realizing she'd been divulging private information to a complete stranger. "Why are you asking about Louis?"

I leaned against the counter and said in a low voice, "I'm the one who found Mr. Mahoney's body. I saw the basket from Brenda on his desk."

"You found him? Was he still alive when you discovered him?" Terri scooted as close as she could get to the reception counter. She'd gone from suspicious to oddly concerned about her boss. She looked up at me, and I felt the eagerness in her intense gaze. "Did he say anything to you about me? I feel so bad that I had a dentist appointment and wasn't here when he needed me." I could hear the hope in her voice.

I gave her a strange look. "No, sorry. He was already gone when I got there."

"Oh." Her face fell, and she pushed her chair back from the counter, suddenly all business. "Well, no one said anything about a donation to a preschool auction."

"Is there someone else who might know? We were really excited about this donation and would still love to get it."

"My other boss. Dorinda Lang." She sneered the words. "She'll know."

For all the information I was getting out of Terri, I might as well have been talking to Mikey. I tried my hardest to be polite. I wasn't aware of there being another owner at Ericksville Espresso, but that explained the second office door. "Ok, is Ms. Lang in today?"

"She'll be in later."

"Can you tell me what time she'll be back?"

She rolled her eyes, clicked the mouse a few times on her computer, then looked up at me. "Looks like she's out until three today."

"Great." I smiled at her. "I'll come back later. Thanks for all your help."

"Uh huh." She turned back to her computer, and I left the office.

While I'd been unsuccessful in obtaining the auction basket, I had learned quite a bit about Louis Mahoney. Although his secretary seemed to be fond of him, he'd been a serial cheater. He'd probably gained plenty of enemies through his extramarital affairs. If his wife had known about any of them, she'd be a good suspect.

I'd come back later in the day and talk to his business partner, Dorinda. Maybe she'd have some more intel on who would want to kill Louis.

~

As promised, Beth had left the contact names for the last-minute wedding on my desk. The catering information had been completed, but I had a few questions for her before I called the client to confirm details.

I knocked on the half-closed door to her office. She came to the door and opened it slightly, holding her index finger to her mouth.

"Shh. Ella's asleep."

I glanced in the corner of the room to where Beth had set up a small Pack 'n Play. My daughter was sleeping peacefully with her thumb stuck in her mouth.

Beth came out of the room and shut the door behind her. "What's up? Did you find the wedding folder I put on your desk?"

I nodded. "Actually, I had some questions about it." I pointed at the catering information on the client intake form. "Is this the total finalized number of attendees? Or are they allowed to change it later?" Usually we gave clients up until a week before the event date to change their catering order, but with this one being so last-minute, I wasn't sure if Beth had let them bend the rules a little.

"Oh, right. I did tell them they had until tomorrow to give us a final count."

"And they're paying the regular weekday fee, right?"

"Yes, but I'm not charging them anything extra for the smaller room where they'll have the ceremony. I may have forgotten to include that."

I made a note of the appropriate fees on the form. "Ok, thanks. I'll give them a call now. Thanks for watching Ella."

"No problem." She smiled at me and returned to her office.

I dialed the client's phone number, and someone answered on the first ring.

"Hello?" a woman said in an excited voice.

"Hi, is this Lila?"

"Yes, this is she."

"This is Jill Andrews from the Boathouse Event Center. I'm going to be coordinating your wedding."

"I thought I recognized the phone number on the caller ID. Thanks again for squeezing us into your schedule."

"Of course." I went over the details with the client and let her know they needed to give us final catering numbers by the next day. "Is there anything else you need?"

"Well ..." She hesitated. "I've always wanted to release a pair of doves at our wedding. Do you think that's possible?"

Doves? We'd had some clients do that previously, but we usually had to place an order weeks earlier for the birds.

"I'll pay extra. Do you think we can do it?"

"Uh, I'm not sure. I'll have to check and see if I can get them in time."

"Oh, that would be wonderful. Most of my family won't be able to attend the wedding since it's so last minute, and it's not the huge formal wedding I've dreamed about since I was a little girl, but I didn't want to wait any longer to marry Eddie. But I thought maybe I could have a touch of my plans for a fancy wedding by releasing doves to symbolize our bond." She sighed. "We'll be separated by distance, but not in our hearts."

I closed my eyes. She had it bad. "I'll see what I can do. We can discuss it tomorrow when you give me the final counts."

"I'll call you tomorrow afternoon. Thank you so much—you have no idea how much this means to me," she gushed.

"Of course, that's what we're here for—to make your wedding day special."

Doves. Of course she wanted doves. The simple weekday wedding had suddenly become more complicated—something I didn't have time for. I sighed. I had promised her I'd try to make her wedding wish come true, so it was time to call around for a pair of white doves.

The first place I tried laughed at me when I made the request. I was getting down to the bottom of my short list of bird suppliers in the Seattle area when I finally found one with availability.

"Sure, we can bring them over Tuesday afternoon." The man took my details and said goodbye.

"Thank you so much."

I hung up the phone and put the folder for the client's wedding on the side of my desk before reviewing the details for the weekend's events. I'd been working on both the Saturday and Sunday events—a wedding and a college graduation party. After a careful review of both events, I concluded everything was set to go. I wasn't scheduled to be on-site for the weekend, something I was profoundly grateful for. I needed to get some time away from the office.

I checked the clock on my computer. Almost three. Time to meet Louis Mahoney's business partner, Dorinda Lang. Perhaps I'd be able to get some information from her about enemies of Louis but, if nothing else, I hoped she would know where I could find the auction basket.

Beth's office door was open, and Ella was lying on her back, staring at a cloth sunflower with a shiny mirror that was attached to the side of the Pack 'n Play.

"Hey, I was going to head out for an hour or so. I still haven't located that auction donation from Ericksville Espresso. The co-owner is supposed to be there today after three and, with any luck, she'll know where it is. Do you mind watching Ella?"

"She'll be content to watch herself in that mirror for the next hour. It seems to be her favorite toy." Beth looked at her granddaughter with adoration. "She's such a good girl."

I smiled, then waved at Ella and said goodbye to Beth.

7

The flashy red car I'd seen earlier at Ericksville Espresso was gone, but an older model Jeep had taken its place and the parking near the warehouse side was full. I pulled into a parking spot next to the Jeep and went inside. The lights were off in the reception area, and Terri wasn't behind her desk. The front door had been unlocked, so I figured someone was there, but it was eerily similar to the day I'd found Louis's body.

"Hello?" I called out. No one answered.

Light leaked from under the door, so I pushed the door to the warehouse open. Today, there were workers bagging coffee and moving pallets against a wall with a forklift. I walked toward Dorinda's office, carefully averting my eyes from the office where I'd found the body.

The door was closed, but I could hear someone inside talking on the phone. I knocked, and a female voice said, "Come in."

The office was decorated in a less formal fashion than Louis's private domain. The hardwood floors in here were covered with a soft gray rug, and the lines of the antique wooden desk were much more feminine.

The familiar-looking woman behind the desk said goodbye to whomever she was talking to on the phone and folded her hands in front of her on the desk, a puzzled expression on her face.

"Hi," she said.

"Hi." I held out my hand. "I'm Jill Andrews from Busy Bees Preschool."

"Is something wrong with Daniel?" Her face blanched, and she straightened in the chair, her eyes wild.

As soon as she said her son's name, I realized where I knew her from. She was the biter's mom, the one who'd apologized to me when her son kicked Mikey in the preschool lobby. From her tone, it was obvious she thought I'd come there because her son had been injured or was in trouble.

"Oh gosh, no. Sorry to worry you. I'm not here about Daniel."

The tension evaporated from her body, and some color returned to her cheeks. "You had me worried. No one from the preschool has ever shown up here before." She eyed me. "You're Mikey's mom, right?"

"I am. I'm actually here because Louis had promised to donate an Ericksville Espresso basket for the upcoming preschool auction. I stopped in earlier, but Terri didn't know anything about it. She suggested I come back later and ask you about it."

She rolled her eyes when I mentioned Terri. "Terri wouldn't know where to find something even if it bit her on the rear. I don't even know where she went today; she hasn't been around for hours."

I smiled at her. "I was hoping you knew where I could find the auction donation?"

"Of course." She got up and opened a closet I hadn't noticed in one corner of the office. She turned and presented me with a plastic-wrapped basket about the height of a king-size pillow. "It's right here."

I reached out for the basket. "Wow, it's gorgeous." The dark woven basket was wrapped with opaque purple plastic wrap, and a fancy purple bow had been tied at the top. Inside, there were several bags of coffee beans, two mugs, a small coffee grinder, and a single-serve espresso machine. "This will be very popular."

She smiled. "Glad we could help." She ran her fingers over the curled ends of the bow. "I loved putting it together."

"Well, you did a great job." I admired the basket.

"Oh, I didn't wrap it, Louis's wife did, but I chose the contents. Louis was the one who recommended Busy Bees Preschool to me when Daniel and I moved to Ericksville."

"Are you not from around here?"

"No. We're originally from up north in Bellton, but after Daniel's father died last year, I used some of his life insurance money to purchase half of Ericksville Espresso. My husband's parents live nearby in Everton, and I wanted a fresh start for my son and I."

"I'm so sorry for your loss." I rested the edge of the heavy basket on the top of a chair. "How long have you lived here?"

"Only a few months." She pressed her lips together. "It's been hard for Daniel with moving to a new place and new school. I know he misses his old friends and neighbors, and especially his dad. I have to admit, it's been a hard transition for me too."

Poor kid. He was too young to have experienced such a painful loss. No wonder he was having trouble at school.

When Adam had been traveling a lot a few months ago, Mikey had been in trouble several times at school. I couldn't even imagine how horrible it would be for all of us if something happened to Adam. And for Daniel, it was even worse as he had moved to a new town and had to start all over again with friends. Inspiration struck.

"We should have a playdate sometime. I'm sure Mikey and Daniel would have a great time together once they get to know each other."

"Really? You'd be willing to do that?" Her eyes widened. "I know Daniel has had problems with the other kids at school."

"Yeah, it will be fine. Are you free on Sunday?"

She checked her calendar and nodded.

"Great! How about one o'clock?"

"That would be wonderful."

I gave her my address and crossed my fingers that I could convince Mikey that a playdate would be fun. Daniel needed to have a fair shot at making friends at his new school, and it seemed like Dorinda could use a friend too.

"So how did you end up here?" I swept my hand across her office.

"I've always wanted to own a business and, after working in the food industry for most of my life, this was a natural fit. I heard through the grapevine that Louis was selling half of the company, so I bought it. Plus, Ericksville looked like a nice place to live."

"It is." I smiled at her. "Well, we're glad you moved here. How do you like it?"

"Eh." She shrugged. "I like the town, but I'm starting to have regrets about purchasing this business."

"Because of Louis's death?"

"No, it started before that." She crossed the room to sit

down at her desk and gestured for me to have a seat in the chair across from her. "Do you want some coffee?"

"I'm good, but thanks." I set the gift basket on the floor and took a seat. "So if not because of Louis, why do you regret the purchase?"

"Well, it was because of Louis, but not because of his death." She gazed at me. "I probably shouldn't be talking about this, but I could really use someone to talk to." Her eyes teared up. "I really miss my husband sometimes."

I touched her hand which rested on the desk and offered her a Kleenex out of my purse. "It's ok. I'm glad to be able to help you. This has been a tough year for you."

She nodded gratefully and took the tissue. "I researched the business before I purchased it. I knew it had some financial issues, but they weren't insurmountable. They got worse soon after I bought into it."

"How so?" I prodded.

"Louis was always taking money out of the business. His wife, Sandy, is a shopaholic, and it takes a lot to support her. Maybe once upon a time when the business was thriving, that would have been fine, but now, not so much ..." She dabbed her eyes and blew her nose. "With my financial knowledge and background in the food industry, I'd hoped to be able to turn the place around. After Louis's death, I went over our financials again, and things are getting worse. He's run the business into the ground. We'd agreed on sharing the profits, but I never expected him to take out so much, so soon." She stared past me at the door to the warehouse before whispering, "I'm going to have to lay off some of the workers soon if we don't start making more money."

I fidgeted in my seat. I didn't know what to say, so I just sat there, waiting for her to talk again.

"I hate to say it, but now that Louis is dead and I have

the chance to purchase his share of the business, I may be able to make Ericksville Espresso profitable again." She looked at me. "I sound like a horrible person, don't I?"

"No, no. I understand what you mean." Losing all the money from her husband's life insurance proceeds in this investment would be devastating for her and Daniel. But was it enough of a motive for her to kill Louis? I didn't want to think ill of Dorinda as I was starting to really like her, but I needed to prevent that from coloring my objectivity. "I don't know if you knew this, but my sister-in-law and I were the ones who found Louis when we came for the auction basket earlier in the week."

"No, I didn't." She stared at me wide-eyed. "I'm so sorry you had to go through that. It must have been awful to find him like that." She shuddered.

"It wasn't something I ever want to go through again. Such a tragedy. Did you know he was allergic to peanuts?"

"Yes, of course. He told everyone he met and was extremely careful about what he ate. He religiously kept an EpiPen in the very front of his desk, but he must not have been able to access it before he fell unconscious. Last week, I grabbed a pen out of his office, and he freaked out when I told him I'd gone in that drawer. He immediately pulled it out to check that it was still there and easily accessible." Tears filled her eyes. "I hadn't known him long, but no one deserved to die like that. I wish I'd been here and could have helped, but I'd already left to pick up Daniel from school."

I nodded. Something she said struck me as odd though. When Desi and I found the body, the desk drawers had been open, and the contents strewn across the floor. I didn't remember seeing an EpiPen anywhere there. It was possible that he'd used it previously or it had expired and he hadn't bothered to replace the device, but that didn't seem likely considering Dorinda's comment about how careful he was about his life-threatening allergy. Had whoever murdered Louis removed the EpiPen from his desk drawer?

Dorinda leaned toward me. "Do you think Brenda Watkins had anything to do with it? I heard they were asking her questions about Louis. I've met her at school, and she seems like someone who wouldn't hurt a fly. I have to admit I was surprised to hear she was dating Louis."

I shook my head. "No, I've been friends with her for a while, and there's no way she would have killed him."

"But I heard they were having an affair. Maybe she found out she wasn't the only woman he was seeing?"

"Terri mentioned something similar—that this wasn't the first time Louis had cheated on his wife. Maybe the woman he was with before Brenda had something to do with his murder?"

She fiddled with a pen on her desk, threading it between her fingers. "Funny that Terri was the one who told you that. When I first moved here, she and Louis were hot and heavy."

"Really." That would explain Terri's overly concerned attitude about her boss's death. "Are you sure?"

"Oh yeah. I found them together in his office one time." She grimaced. "I learned to always knock after that."

"Hmm. And his wife didn't know?"

"Not that I knew. I was new here, and I didn't think it was my place to tell her. I didn't know he was dating Brenda." She glanced at the clock. "I should probably finish up the work I need to get done today. Daniel is with a sitter, but I promised I'd be back by five thirty."

I stood. "I understand. Thanks for the gift basket. Are you planning on going to the auction next Friday?"

"I am. I hear it's an aviation theme?"

"It is." I grinned and told her a little about the auction. One of the parents at the preschool loved flying and had donated some of his flying memorabilia. The main room of the Boathouse would be decorated like an airport hangar, and the auction dinner tickets were printed as boarding passes.

"It sounds fun. I'm looking forward to it. I'll give Daniel my boarding pass to play with after the auction. He loves anything having to do with airplanes."

Before leaving, I said, "I'm looking forward to our play-date on Sunday. Let me know if you need help finding our house."

"I will. It was so nice to officially meet you, Jill." She waved at me. "See you then."

I returned the wave and exited her office. Before I left the building, an idea came to me. I popped my head back into Dorinda's office.

"Excuse me, but in all the commotion of finding Louis dead, I somehow lost an earring. Would it be ok if I go in his office to look for it?"

"Sure, go ahead. The police have already removed anything they needed for their investigation. If you don't find it there, you might want to ask if they have it."

"Thanks. It isn't a big deal if I don't find it, but I figured as long as I was here already, I'd take a look." I left her alone in her office and entered the office next door. The masculine furnishings—so different from those in Dorinda's office— gave me flashbacks to the evening Desi and I discovered Louis's body.

I hadn't really lost my earring, but when we were there before, things had been chaotic and I hadn't mentally processed much of the scene of his death. Was it possible there was something there that the police might have missed?

I scanned the room. Everything seemed to be how it had been the last time I'd been there.

"Excuse me. What are you doing in here?"

I turned. A tall man stared down at me. Judging from his attire, he worked in the warehouse.

"Uh ..." Words eluded me. "I'm, uh, looking for an earring I lost in here when I met with Mr. Mahoney earlier in the week. Dorinda said it was ok to be here." I got down on all fours on the floor and made a show of looking under the desk. I swept my hand across the rug and looked up at the worker.

He looked at me with suspicion but put his hands in his pocket and pivoted around to go back to the warehouse. I was about to get up when I noticed something odd.

A thick, pen-like object was stuck in the tracks underneath the middle desk drawer. I grabbed my keys and used the penlight on the keychain to see better. It was the missing EpiPen. How did it get all the way back there if he kept it at the front of the drawer? It was possible that he'd somehow jammed it to the back, but that didn't jive with Dorinda's description of how careful he was with it. If the police hadn't noticed it earlier, they probably would think I was crazy to think it suspicious.

I scrambled out from under the desk, grabbed the gift basket from where I'd left it on the floor and wandered out the door in a daze. I was so lost in thought that I accidentally wandered out on to the warehouse floor.

"Hey, lady!" a man shouted. "I almost ran you over."

I looked up to see a yellow forklift stopped just in front of me. "Sorry." I shivered at the close call and scurried over to the pathway along the wall, making my way out to my minivan. Terri still wasn't back when I passed the reception desk.

Things were certainly a mess at Ericksville Espresso. It seemed like ages ago that Desi and I had been excited to see the inside of the building. Now that I knew the tangled web of its inhabitants, I had no desire to ever go back there.

8

_____

On Saturday, I brought the kids over to Desi's house to play so I could go in to work for a few hours at the Boathouse. I'd hoped to not have to work over the weekend, but I needed to check on a few things.

As soon as we got to her house, Mikey ran off to play with Anthony, leaving his aunt, myself, and the babies alone in the living room. I held Lina while Desi bounced Ella on her knee.

"How are you doing?" she asked.

"I'm fine," I said automatically.

She peered at me. "No you're not. C'mon. I can tell when something's wrong."

"It's the auction and Louis's murder and Adam not being here. When the auction is over, my stress levels will go down."

"Do you need help with it?"

"No, it's all taken care of. I feel like I did with my wedding though. You plan and worry about all the details, and then it's finally the big day. Afterward, you're just grateful that it's finally over with." I knew Desi had a lot on her plate too, and I didn't want to trouble her.

"Got it. Well, if you need anything, please don't hesitate to ask."

"I did—you're watching my kids for me." I grinned at her.

"True." She laughed and waved me off. "Go, get to work. Make this the best auction Busy Bees has ever seen."

I'd left my phone in the car, and the screen showed a missed call. I checked the log. My parents. With all the commotion over Louis's murder, I'd forgotten to return my mom's phone call. *Again.* I tapped the button to call them back, hit speakerphone, then drove toward the Boathouse.

"Hi, Mom," I said when she answered.

"Jill," my mother said warmly over the line. "It's so nice to hear from you."

"You too. Adam told me you called, but this has been a crazy week. I'm sorry I didn't call you back sooner."

"Don't worry about it, honey. We know you've been busy. Your dad and I were just wondering about when we should come for Mikey's birthday party. It's still next Sunday, right?"

I froze despite the warmth trapped in my car. *Oh no.* How had I managed to forget Mikey's fourth birthday? I vaguely remembered discussing it with my mother a few months ago and making plans for a party next Sunday. Unfortunately, that was as far as I'd gotten on party planning.

"Uh, yes. One o'clock." My mind spun, trying to work out everything I'd need to do. Invitations, party guests, food, decorations. How would I possibly get everything done? It didn't escape me that I'd been too busy planning other people's events to remember my own son's birthday. "I'll get the guest room ready for you."

"Oh no. You don't have to do that. We've already made

plans to stay in a hotel in Ericksville. We don't want to inconvenience you."

"Are you sure? It's no trouble."

"Yes, honey," she said. "It'll be easier for everyone."

They always stayed at my house. I knew I should be relieved that I didn't need to get the guest room ready, but something felt off.

"We're planning on coming out on Wednesday." Her voice caught a little. "We have something important to discuss with you, so maybe we can get together the next day."

She sounded serious. I pulled over and held the phone to my ear.

"Mom, what's wrong?" A car whizzed by with pop music blaring out the open windows.

"We'd rather tell you in person."

"Are you ok? Is Dad?"

She hesitated for a moment. "We're fine. But we need to talk with you. Can you do Thursday morning?"

I checked my phone calendar. I could move some things around.

"Sure. Does ten o'clock work? I can meet you at the hotel with the kids. I know Mikey will be excited to see you both."

"We're looking forward to seeing them as well. That's perfect. We'll be at the Sunset Hotel. Just give me a call when you arrive."

After she hung up the phone, I stayed parked for a few minutes. Even though Mom had said she and Dad were fine, something was definitely wrong. I tried to push it out of my mind though as I still had some things to take care of at the Boathouse. The clients for the Tuesday wedding had called with a last-minute change to the guest list and needed to decrease their catering count, so I fired off an e-mail to our catering manager, Lizzie, to let her know. Then, I checked on the wedding reception set-up. Things were going smoothly, so I worked on more auction details and then returned to Desi's house to pick up the kids.

"You look like something the cat dragged in," were the first words out of her mouth.

I glared at her. "Thanks a lot."

"What's going on? More auction drama?"

"No. My parents are coming to town for Mikey's birthday party next Sunday."

"Mikey's birthday party?" She cocked her head to the side. "I don't remember getting an invitation."

"That's because I forgot." I grimaced.

"Oh. So what are you going to do for Mikey's birthday?"

Ugh. I needed to figure that out ASAP if I wanted anyone to show up next weekend. I'd have to bake a cake, buy decorations, and decide whom to invite. That last item was a big sticking point with me right now.

"Did I tell you that Dorinda is a parent of one of the kids at Busy Bees preschool?"

"No, which one? In Mikey and Anthony's class?"

"Yes, Daniel." I waited for her reaction and wasn't disappointed.

Her mouth gaped open. "He's the one who's been biting Anthony, isn't he?"

"They told you who it was that bit Anthony?" I was surprised as the school wasn't allowed to disclose anything about a student to anyone other than their parents.

She scoffed. "Of course not. All I got from them was, 'a friend of Anthony's' did it. A *friend*—ha! But I asked Anthony, and he told me it was Daniel. It's not the first time he's complained about Daniel hurting him or his friends."

I sighed. "I know, I hear the same thing from Mikey, but

Daniel has gone through a lot. When I went to Ericksville Espresso again to pick up the auction basket, I met Daniel's mother, Dorinda. Turns out she's a co-owner. Anyway, his dad died recently and they moved down here from Bellton, which is probably why he's so unhappy. But I don't think most of the kids like him, Mikey included. Daniel is coming over tomorrow for a playdate, and I'm hoping to change Mikey's opinion, but no guarantees. Do you think it would be ok for me to invite him to the birthday party?"

She frowned. "Are you inviting all the other kids in Mikey's class?"

"Yes."

"Well, you definitely have to invite him." She stared at me. "I get it, I'm not keen on Anthony being bitten either. But if you invite all the other kids, you can't leave Daniel out. And it sounds like he's had a rough time. We'll just keep a close eye on everyone at the party."

My shoulders slumped, and I gulped my coffee, the mild burning sensation distracting me from my problems for a moment. "Ok. What about Nancy's daughter? Do I have to invite her?"

"As much as I don't want to spend any more time with Nancy than absolutely necessary, you have to invite her kid too."

"Do you think if I invite people now, they'd be able to come to a party on Sunday?"

"Uh ..." She looked at me. "Do you want the truth?"

"I know. I should have done it earlier, but I was overwhelmed with everything else and forgot." My spirits rose. "On the bright side, if I send out invitations now, maybe not everyone in his class will be able to come. Twenty kids and their parents would be an awful lot of people in my house at one time." I changed the subject. "Something is going on with my parents. My mom said they're coming into town on Wednesday, but they're staying in a hotel."

"Well maybe they wanted to stay out of your way."

"That's what my mom said, but she also said they need to talk to me about something. She wouldn't say what." I twisted my wedding ring around my finger. "Desi, what if it's something bad? Like one of them is sick or something?"

She put her hand on my arm. "I'm sure everything is ok. Besides, you'll see them soon. Don't work yourself up before then. Do you want to stay for dinner?"

"I think I just want to go home." I felt more weary than I could ever remember feeling in the past.

"Ok, I'll get the boys." She walked to the entrance to the hallway.

"Mikey!" she shouted. "Your mom is here."

The boys thundered in, coming to a halt in front of Desi.

"Can Mikey stay for dinner?" Anthony begged.

She ruffled his hair. "No, I think Aunt Jill wants to go home." Her eyes met mine, and I nodded.

At the door, she hugged me again. "It will all work out, I promise."

Although I didn't feel up to it, I didn't want to cancel the playdate I'd scheduled with Dorinda. While I felt like my life was falling apart from stress, Daniel's world truly had been shattered and I wanted to help him and Dorinda in any way I could.

"Mom," Mikey whined. "Do we have to have them over?"

"Yes." I glared at him and arranged some carrots, celery sticks, and ranch dip on a platter. To sweeten the mood, I placed some of Desi's blondie brownies on a plate. "You have to give Daniel a chance."

"But he's so mean to me and Anthony." He gave me a sad, puppy dog look.

I knelt in front of him. "I know he hasn't been very nice to you in the past, but he's new here and needs friends. You've lived here all your life and have had that time to make friends, right?"

He nodded.

"Well, maybe he doesn't know how to be a good friend. Do you think you could teach him?"

"I guess so." He didn't look convinced, but that was probably the best I was going to get out of him.

"Can you go upstairs and get your boxes of Legos? You boys can play with them down here in the living room while Ella takes her nap." The baby had fallen asleep after fretting for twenty minutes and, even with her door closed, I didn't want to risk having the boys wake her up. Besides, if they were downstairs, Dorinda and I could keep an eye on them better.

He grumbled something and ran up the stairs. I took that as a yes.

The doorbell rang, and I answered it. Dorinda stood next to her son, a pained expression on her face. Daniel seemed about as happy as Mikey was to have this playdate.

"Hey." I motioned for them to come in. "How's it going?"

"Things have been better," she said, staring pointedly at her son before turning back to me. "Here, I brought you some of our most popular coffee." She handed me a one pound sack of ground Willowby Dark Roast.

"Thanks, that is so nice of you. I was thinking about making some coffee. Daniel, you can go play with Mikey."

Mikey tilted his head up at the sound of his name, but he didn't acknowledge his guest.

"Don't forget to share, honey," Dorinda whispered to her son.

Ignoring her, Daniel ran over to the box of Legos Mikey had brought downstairs, and Dorinda followed me into the kitchen and sat on a barstool.

"Have things been that bad?" I prepared the coffee, then sat across from her.

"I don't know what gets into him. I mean, I know he's upset about losing his dad, but he seems so angry."

"Would seeing a counselor help?" The coffee had finished percolating, so I walked over to the coffeepot and filled cups for us. I surreptitiously sniffed my coffee but couldn't discern anything special about it.

"I've made an appointment for him to see someone." She shrugged. "We'll see if it works."

I changed the subject, hoping to take her mind off her son's behavior. "How are things going at work? Did Terri ever come back on Friday?"

She glanced over to the kids, and I followed her gaze. The boys were quietly playing separately on the rug, but at least they had developed a sort of coexistence.

"Yeah, she finally came back, just long enough to tell me she was tendering her resignation. Apparently she wasn't interested in working there after Louis was gone."

"You said before that they had an, um ... intimate relationship. Do you know if she went into his office the evening of his murder?"

She regarded me shrewdly. "You think she may have killed Louis because he had dumped her?"

I shrugged. "She was acting really odd when I was there, and she admitted to seeing the basket from Brenda." To me, it seemed suspicious for Terri to quit right after her boss was murdered.

Dorinda looked lost in thought. "I'm not a huge fan of Terri, but a murderer? I don't know about that. But, yes, I'm sure she was in and out of his office all day, delivering mail and such."

"What about his wife? Did she go in there much?"

She grinned. "I often joked that I wished I had a wife like Sandy. She brought Louis lunch every day at noon, just like clockwork. If he wasn't there, she'd drop it off in his office. So yeah, I'm sure she was in his office that day." She stared at me and twisted her wedding ring around her finger. "I had access to his office, too, as did everyone in the warehouse. It could have been anyone at Ericksville Espresso."

"But not everyone had a motive to kill him."

"No." She sipped her coffee, deep in thought. "I'm sure the police are working on it, but I really hope they figure out who killed him soon." She shivered, despite the warm coffee. "It's a little creepy in there at night now, knowing there's a murderer on the loose."

A commotion over by the fireplace drew our attention.

Daniel was holding on to a Lego car, and Mikey was trying to grab it away from him. They were both standing up and glaring at each other, looking almost comical with their petite statures and character T-shirts. Under their feet, the floor was a minefield of scattered Lego bricks.

"Hey, that's mine," Mikey shouted.

"I had it first!" Daniel dropped to the floor and hunched up in a ball over the car.

Dorinda and I exchanged glances. Up until this point, things had been going reasonably well.

Wah, wah. They had woken the baby. Ella's cries came

over the baby monitor and simultaneously drifted down the stairs.

"I think the playdate may be over." Dorinda gulped the remaining coffee and walked over to her son, dodging the Legos on the floor. "Daniel, it's time to go. We've got to get to Target before dinner time anyway."

"Fine." He threw the toy car on the couch and ran to the door. As his mother gathered their belongings, he bounced from foot to foot on the doormat with a grimace on his face. "Mom, c'mon."

"Sorry," Dorinda said to me with a look of apology. "Maybe things will go better next time?"

I nodded. "They just need to get used to playing with each other. Don't worry about it. When his cousin Anthony comes over, they sometimes argue too. It's totally normal." I glanced over at Mikey, who was studiously ignoring his guest.

"Mikey, say goodbye, please."

"Bye," he uttered without looking up.

Dorinda waved goodbye to me and guided her son out the door. "See you at school," she called over her shoulder.

"See you." I shut the door behind them. Ella must have gone back to sleep because the racket from upstairs had stopped. I walked over to Mikey and sat cross-legged on the floor next to him.

"Mikey."

He didn't look up. I tried again, resting my hand on his shoulder. "Mikey."

"What?"

"Can you please try to be nice to Daniel? He's going through a tough time and could really use a friend. His dad died last year, and I'm sure he misses him."

Mikey appeared to think about it and then looked up at me. "His dad is gone?"

I wasn't sure he understood what death meant, but he did understand what it was like to not have your dad around. "Yes."

He contemplated my response and then said, "I'll try, Mom. Can I play now?"

"Sure. If you want a snack, there's veggies and dip on the counter. I'll make dinner in a little bit."

I went upstairs to check on Ella. She was awake but lying quietly in her crib, staring at the ceiling. She smiled when I picked her up. I sat in the recliner in her room and held her to my chest, staring out the window for a minute.

Although I'd managed to get some information from Dorinda about who had access to the basket with the chocolates in Louis's office, nothing had been cleared up. I'd met Terri, but Sandy was an enigma to me. I needed to find out more about her, but how could I stage a meeting with her without it looking forced?

9

When I went back to work on Monday, I was determined to focus on everything I had to do at the Boathouse. I waded through the e-mails I'd deemed non-priority over the weekend and updated some files on my desk. At noon, I came up for air and let myself relax into my leather desk chair, the one luxury in the office. I closed my eyes.

What would it be like to have a fancy office like the one Louis had at Ericksville Espresso? I didn't want such masculine furnishings, but a nicer desk than the scarred wooden one I'd been using would be nice. I made a note to ask Beth if there was any budget available for office furniture. After all, I met with clients in my office, and I wanted to make a good impression on them.

Had Louis ever met customers in his office? If so, that could add a whole bunch more people onto the list of possible suspects. Thinking about Louis in his office made me remember the sight of his swollen face, and I shuddered. Would I ever be able to get that image out of my head?

Someone knocked on my office door.

"Come in." I scooted my chair closer to my desk.

"Hey, Jill," our catering manager, Lizzie said.

"What's up?

"Well," she said, "I'm a little confused about the food order we received today. The numbers aren't matching up for the total of event attendees."

I groaned. It was always something. We were often shorted food by our suppliers, and I'd have to spend all day trying to fix their mistakes.

"Which events?"

"The wedding tomorrow and then your preschool auction on Friday."

Well that just went from bad to worse. Nancy would never forgive me if things weren't perfect for the preschool auction.

"Ok. What's the issue?"

"There's too much food for the wedding, and we're way under for the auction filet mignon entrees."

"Did you call the supplier and ask them what happened?"

Lizzie turned pink. "I did."

"And what did they say?" I was trying to train the catering staff to problem solve first before coming to me about everything. My first few weeks had consisted of extinguishing one fire after another.

"They said you sent them an e-mail asking for the change."

I raised my eyebrows. "I didn't do that."

She shrugged. "They said you sent them a change order for the beef on Saturday."

My cell phone buzzed, and I pulled it out to check who was calling. Nancy. I wasn't going to deal with her right then, so I let it go to voicemail.

I opened my e-mails and scanned the message I'd sent the supplier on Saturday. I checked the information in the change order with my files on the wedding. The color drained from my face as I ran my finger over the order number.

I'd given them the wrong order number and had accidentally changed our order for the auction from a hundred people to thirty. I'd meant to decrease the wedding's order to thirty from forty. I closed my eyes and rested my head in my hands before looking up at her.

"Are we able to get more filet mignon before the auction?"

"I can ask them. I wanted to find out from you first what the order was supposed to be."

I looked her in the eye. "I'm so sorry, Lizzie. This is all my fault. I'll call the supplier and talk with them. Thanks for bringing this to my attention."

Nancy called again, and again I punched the button to send her to voicemail. Irrationally, I wondered if she'd somehow found out that I'd messed up the entree order. My stress levels shot up even higher. She would kill me if the catering wasn't exactly as she requested. Was I going to have to drive to our supplier in Seattle and buy more filet mignon for the auction? How much would that even cost?

How could I have made such a big mistake? The effects of all the stressors in my life were coming out. I'd changed the beef order right after the ominous phone call with my mother. Normally, I could handle that type of thing and stay calm, but with taking care of the kids by myself, managing the auction preparations, and trying to help figure out who had really killed Louis, it was too much. Had I made a mistake in going back to work? Who knew what mistakes I'd make in the future.

I was spiraling and needed to send myself on a time-out. I sat on the floor of my office with my back pressed up against the wall and closed my eyes to meditate. After a few moments of blissful quiet, my mind was clear enough to call the supplier and attempt to fix my error.

Before calling our beef supplier, I double- and triple-checked the correct number of guests for each event. When I was satisfied that I had accurate numbers on the notepad in front of me, I dialed the supplier. The receptionist there directed me to the manager. Crossing my fingers, I explained my mistake.

He chuckled. "Sure, we can get you more filet mignon by Friday. But it's going to cost a little more because our normal delivery day to you is on Monday, and we'll have to make a special stop to get it there by the end of the week." He quoted me the amount for the extra charge. "I won't be able to cut your other order though. We've already delivered that quantity."

I breathed a sigh of relief. We could find a use for the wedding overage, but the auction entrees had been the big problem. The extra cost for the auction wasn't nearly as bad as I'd expected. "No problem. Thank you so much."

"You're very welcome," he said pleasantly before hanging up.

I entered the extra delivery fee for the auction's dinner entrees on the spreadsheet I used to track each event's individual expenses. The additional charge would significantly cut into the minimal margin for the event, but at least it wasn't going to sink it. I wasn't looking forward to telling Beth though. She always seemed to have everything together in her life, and I didn't want to tell her I couldn't handle the pressure.

~

When I'd finally worked up the nerve to tell Beth about the whole filet mignon snafu, I knocked on her door.

"Come in," she sang out.

I heard Ella giggling from inside the room.

"Hey," I said. Beth had Ella sitting on her desk in front of her and was jiggling her legs, pretending she was dancing.

She looked surprised to see me. "Do you need help with something? I thought you'd have left to go get Mikey by now."

I looked at my watch. Shoot, she was right. I did need to get him soon. There wasn't any time to dillydally with telling her. I took a deep breath and spit it out.

"Beth. I messed up."

Her head bobbed up sharply. "What's wrong?"

"I accidentally cut the order for the auction entrees in half. Well, by more than half." I held my breath. I didn't think she'd be mad, but I didn't want her to be disappointed in me either.

She raised an eyebrow. "How did that happen?"

"I mixed up the event numbers for the wedding on Tuesday and the preschool auction and requested the wrong order be changed."

"Ok. Well, did you call the supplier?"

"I did. They said they could increase our order, but since they have to make an unplanned delivery to us, they need to charge an extra fee." I told her the amount of the additional delivery charge. "I'm really sorry Beth. I don't know what happened. I changed the order from home on Saturday, and I must have been so upset about finding Louis Mahoney's body last week and some personal things that I wasn't careful enough."

She waved her hand dismissively. "Don't worry about it. Things happen. It's fixed now, and it didn't cost us too much more."

I hung my head. "I'll work extra to make up for it."

She put Ella back in her Pack 'n Play and crossed the room to where I stood in the doorway. "Honey, don't worry about it. I'm serious. This kind of thing happens all the time."

"To you?" I was near tears now.

"Of course. You don't think I've been in this business for so long and never made a mistake, do you?"

"I guess not." Sometimes it was strange working for my in-laws, but at least they were kind and understanding people.

"I remember one time when Lincoln double-booked the main hall and scheduled two weddings at the same time. We didn't realize the mistake until both wedding parties arrived an hour before the wedding."

My eyes widened. "He did? What did he do?"

"We scrambled to get one of the other rooms ready before the guests showed up. Luckily, one of the weddings wasn't too big, and we were able to fit them into one of the smaller rooms. The bride wasn't happy, but after we offered them a fifty percent discount on the whole wedding and catering fee, they accepted the alternate venue. It was still a little confusing having two weddings going on at the same time." She laughed. "A few of the attendees didn't realize they were in the wrong room until the groom walked up to the altar."

She scanned my face. "You look like there's something on your mind other than the ordering issue. Do you want to talk about it?"

I leaned against the wall. "It's my parents." It felt good to let it out. I hadn't been able to talk to Adam since the odd conversation with my mother the day before. "They're coming out in a few days for Mikey's birthday, and they have something important to tell me, but they won't say what. It's driving me crazy."

"Oh." She smiled at me. "I think you're worrying about nothing. I'm sure everything will be fine."

"I guess. It's not just that though. I've been having second thoughts about working at the Boathouse. I've been working more hours than I'd expected, and it's taking a toll on our family life." I thought about the dishes piling up in the sink and the mound of laundry waiting for me at home. While I wasn't the best housekeeper in the world, I usually hadn't let it get to that point.

Beth frowned. "You didn't say anything, so we didn't know. We can decrease your hours if you'd like. I'd hate to see you quit." Ella cried and Beth picked her up, holding her close. She kissed the top of her head then looked into my eyes. "Lincoln and I love seeing you and the kids every day. But I understand how complicated it can be juggling home and work responsibilities. When my children were little, I went through the same thing as you." A far-off look came into her eyes. "There was always so much to do here and at home."

"So what did you do?" I wiped away the small tears pooling in the corners of my eyes.

"I did what I had to do. Take care of both home and work. It wasn't easy, and you'll never be perfect, but you just do the best you can do." She danced a little with Ella. "You're good at this job, and I think you like it, right?"

I nodded. "I do. I think I'm just letting the stress get to me."

"I think so too. Let's talk about this after the auction is over, ok?" She smiled at me.

"Ok." I checked my watch. "Beth, I've got to go get Mikey. Thanks for reassuring me about the ordering error and the other stuff. I appreciate it."

She hugged me with one arm. "I'll bring Ella over to your house after work, ok?"

"Thanks." I returned to my office, grabbed my purse and locked up before leaving for the preschool.

10

$\mathcal{B}$renda was at the preschool when I arrived to get Mikey. She stood outside the door, as if psyching herself up to go in. She shot me an apprehensive look as I approached the door.

"I don't think anyone in there bites." I laughed. "Well, maybe that isn't quite true. Those gerbils have given me the evil eye before."

She gave me a weak smile. "Brad dropped the kids off at preschool this morning after his weekend with them, so I haven't had to deal with Nancy yet. You know, after everything that happened last week."

I patted her arm. "It'll be ok. I promise."

She looked at me dubiously but followed me inside.

"I'll go get Mikey and the girls if you want to stay here."

She nodded and leaned against the wall. "Thanks."

I figured if she stayed in the lobby, there would be less chance of running into Nancy. Luckily for her, that was true. Unluckily for me, that was because I literally ran into Nancy in the hallway.

Mikey was in his classroom, but he hadn't yet retrieved

his backpack from the hooks in the bathroom hallway. He was busy in the building center, intent on pounding a nail into a stack of wood, alongside his cousin Anthony.

"Backpack?" I asked. "It's time to go."

"I'm almost done, Mom."

I sighed. "I'll get it for you." I hurried into the hallway, not paying attention to where I was going and ran smack into Nancy.

After I bumped into her, she stepped back and curled up her lips. "Please watch where you're going. There are small children in here."

"Sorry, I should have been more careful."

"Yes, you should have." She eyed me with disdain, then said, "And you haven't returned my phone calls. I need to speak with you about the catering choices and—"

I cut her off. "The catering order is set. I'm sorry, but we aren't able to make any more changes at this late a date. Now if you'll excuse me, I need to find my son."

She sputtered, then spun around and exited the hallway into a side classroom.

I found Sara and Dara, and retrieved their backpacks as well.

With the girls in tow, I walked past Mikey, snagging his arm with a free hand. "Let's go."

He protested but came along with me and the girls.

In the lobby, Brenda was still leaning against a wall, looking like she wished she could blend in with the paint. Sara and Dara ran to her, and she hugged them before flashing me a smile. When we were safely outside, she asked me, "Do you want to come over for some coffee? This past weekend was pretty lonely without the girls, and I'd love some company."

I considered her offer. Ella would be with her grandmother

for a couple more hours, so I had time. Plus, I wanted to find out if Brenda had been in Louis's office on the day of his murder.

"Sure, that sounds great."

We made arrangements to meet at her house in twenty minutes. Mikey and I had to walk home to get the car as Brenda's house was on the other side of town.

"Are they going to have any toys for boys to play with?" He strained his head to look at me in the rearview mirror on the way to Brenda's house.

"I'm sure they'll have something," I reassured him. "Maybe even Legos."

"Ok." He leaned his head back against the car seat and stared out the window.

We pulled into Brenda's driveway and parked behind the minivan that she used as her run-about-town car. She also owned a nice white sedan that she used for her real estate business, but she kept that in the garage, safe from children's sticky fingers.

Dara flung the door open as we approached the house. "Hi!" she said brightly. "Mommy is making cookies. Chocolate chip this time." She grinned and ran back inside.

"Cool," Mikey said, and ran ahead to follow her inside.

By the time I got to the kitchen, only thirty seconds later, they each had a chocolate chip cookie stuffed in their mouths.

"It's ok for him to have one, right?" Brenda asked. She held a spatula in one hand and an oven mitt in the other.

"It's fine." I wasn't too particular about the amount of sweets he ate, as long as he still ate his veggies too.

"How did you have time to make cookies already?" I glanced at the clock on the wall. "You've only been home for fifteen minutes, max."

"A sheet of premade cookies." She winked. "A mother's best friend."

"Ah." That explained it. I wasn't much of a baker, so I'd made my share of refrigerated take and bake cookies.

"I started coffee but haven't had a chance to finish it." She gestured with the spatula to the coffeepot.

"I can do it if you'd like," I offered. "After the day I've had, I'd love a cup of coffee."

"That would be great. Can you get the cinnamon out of the spice cupboard? I like to put a dash of it in with the coffee grounds. Gives it a little extra flavor."

I nodded and opened cupboards until I found one that contained spices. A combination of aromas wafted out of the cupboard as I reached for the cinnamon, my hand grazing something that was spilled on the bottom of the cabinet. I picked up the bottle that sat in the sticky mess. Peanut extract. I looked from the bottle to Brenda and back again. She had her back turned to me as she finished arranging the cookies on a plate.

Was it weird that she had peanut extract in her cupboard? It was completely possible that someone could have injected the chocolates that had killed Louis with peanut extract. I'd never met anyone who'd bought it before, but I did remember one of her daughters talking about how her Mom had made peanut butter cookies earlier in the week. Maybe she'd used it in that recipe.

"Hey," I said.

She turned toward me, holding the plate of cookies, with a big, happy homemaker smile on her face.

I held up the peanut extract. "Do you use this in your peanut butter cookies? I wonder if it would kick up the peanut flavor if I used them in my cookies."

"I do. Just a few drops and the whole flavor profile intensifies."

I debated asking my next question, but decided to go for it. "Do you think it would be easy to inject the extract into candy?"

"I don't know about injecting it. It would be pretty strong." She shrugged. "But I guess you could." She narrowed her eyes at me and set the plate down on the counter. "Wait a minute." She shot a glance at the kids and lowered her voice. "Do you think *I* had something to do with Louis's death? I told you I didn't do it."

I'm not the best of liars, and I scrambled to figure out how to answer her question. "No, of course not. It just seemed like using peanut extract would be an easy thing to inject into the chocolates." I eyed her. "Besides, you didn't know he was allergic to peanuts, right?"

She reddened and squirmed a little.

"You did know, didn't you?" I found myself backing away from her.

"I did, but I swear it wasn't me who killed him. On our first date, I suggested Thai food, but he didn't want to risk it because of the peanut oil and peanuts that are common in Thai cooking. He was always so careful and checked the ingredients on everything before he ate it."

"Why didn't you tell me you knew about his allergy?"

Brenda pointed to the small glass bottle of peanut extract. "Because then it would give you and everyone else another reason to think that I killed him." Her voice became teary as she spoke. She swiped at her face and then held the plate up toward the kids.

In a loud voice, she asked, "More cookies, kids?" She flashed them a smile.

They nodded and she brought the full plate over to them before returning to the kitchen.

She looked into my eyes. "I didn't kill him. You believe me, right?"

I didn't answer.

"Whoever killed him knew he had a peanut allergy, but it wasn't me. I would never have hurt him. I really thought things were going well between us."

"Until he died, and you found out he was married."

"Yeah, there was that." Her lips turned downward. "I never suspected he was married. Probably because he told me he was divorced." She leaned against the counter. "How could I have been so stupid? I dated a married man, and now he's dead and I'm a suspect. Karma's coming after me."

She looked like she was hurting so much that I wanted to comfort her. I put my hand on her arm. "It's ok, I believe you." Brenda had been through the wringer in the last week, and I myself had peanuts and peanut butter in my cupboard. That didn't make me a murderer any more than it did Brenda.

With tears in her eyes, she said, "Thank you, Jill. I don't know what I'd do without your friendship."

"No problem. How are things going with Brad? Is he still thinking about moving?"

"Things aren't great with him. He found out that I'm a suspect in Louis's murder, and I just know he's going to request full custody of the girls." Her eyes flickered to her daughters. "I don't know what I'd do without them. He can't move them out of state."

"I'm sure he won't." I pulled her over to the dining room table and scoured the room for anything to distract her from her worries. My eyes landed on a box of cards, laying on a bookshelf. "How about a game of cards?"

She closed her eyes briefly and took a deep breath. "I'd like that."

The dining room table was covered in gift baskets just like the one Brenda had given Louis, minus the love note. A few had the plastic sealed at the top and a wide ribbon emblazoned with her real estate company's name on it across the middle. Others were still missing bottles of wine, which I spotted in boxes underneath the table. They all contained boxes of chocolates, which I fervently hoped didn't contain added peanut extract.

"Pretty," I said.

Brenda smiled. "Yeah, I've found them to be great marketing tools. I try to make them classy and elegant as they represent my brand."

I ran my finger over one of the finished products, the plastic making a pleasant crinkling sound where I touched it. "How do you seal the tops? It looks like the plastic wrap is molded to the basket."

"I use that tool to heat seal it." She gestured to a device perched on one of the chairs. An unplugged electrical cord hung down from it. "It makes the basket look more profes-sional. I tried making those fancy bows, but I'm just not crafty." She moved the baskets to the floor against the wall and we sat down at the table.

"So what's going on with you?" she asked as I dealt the cards.

"Just the auction stuff and work. And trying to juggle all that with family responsibilities." I set the deck down on the table. "How do you do it all?"

She guffawed. "I don't. I try to keep all the balls in the air and then mitigate the damages when I drop one or two."

I stared at her. "But you make it seem so easy. You're always put together, and your kids seem happy."

"They are—well, I hope they are. But I'm not always put together, and you should see my house on a Friday before I can get it cleaned up over the weekend. It usually looks like a tornado went through here." She looked over at her girls. "I just try to do my best, and that's all I can do. Don't be so hard on yourself. The first couple of years after I went back to work weren't easy. It's only been in the last year or so that the systems I've put in place have started to click and things have been easier. Until my unfortunate relationship with Louis, at least." She grimaced. "I never bargained on that. I knew I shouldn't have started dating again, but it had been a couple of years, and I thought it was time I get back out there."

"I'm sorry, Brenda." The corners of my mouth drooped. "You couldn't have known. From what I've heard, he was good at hiding relationships from his wife. He probably did the same with the other women he dated. You are a good mom, and I'll keep your advice in mind, ok?"

She nodded. After a few hands of two-handed pinochle, the tension had evaporated from her shoulders and she laughed genuinely when she won a hand. For a while, she was simply a divorced mother of two little girls and not a murder suspect. For her sake, I wanted to keep it that way.

As promised, Beth dropped Ella off at our house after work. Mikey and I had already eaten dinner, so I fed her some mashed sweet potato and avocado. Mikey was full of questions about everything under the sun, from why Brenda's girls had dark hair and his hair was light to how tall he'd be when he was older. After spending an hour explaining to him that he'd never be six-foot-seven like my sister Becky's husband because his daddy and I weren't extremely tall, I finally had to tell him we'd come back to the discussion later. After bath time and a bedtime story, the kids fell asleep quickly, leaving me alone with my thoughts.

The sweet potato and avocado I'd attempted to feed Ella were now smeared on the dining room floor, but I couldn't make myself get out the steam mop. I'd try to get to it in the next day, but after the week I'd had, I wasn't going to beat myself up if that didn't happen. I should probably do something productive with my time though.

I sat down at my desk, which was built into a long wall in the living room. A few days of mail waited there in a pile for me to sort through. One piece of mail caught my eye—a glossy flyer for an all-inclusive couples resort in Jamaica. We'd spent our honeymoon at a resort in the Caribbean, and Adam kept promising he'd take me back to one for an adults-only getaway, but work always got in the way.

I pulled out my phone and texted him. I didn't know what time zone he was in, but at the moment, I didn't really care if I woke him. Being the kids' only parent for weeks on end wasn't fun.

Hey, how's it going? Do you know when you're coming home? We miss you.

I waited, but there wasn't any answer. Whether he was asleep or avoiding my question, I didn't know. I set my phone down, determined to not be the needy wife.

I picked the Jamaica ad out of the pile. The Londeux Resort. The front of the brochure showcased beautiful white buildings overlooking sandy beaches and impossibly blue water. Room service, couples massages, and swimming with sea turtles. It looked amazing. I stared at the couple on the flipside. They looked so happy. I wanted that to be Adam and me. My eyes teared up. Someday, maybe, it would be.

For now, I could dream about it. I set it aside to bring upstairs so I could look at it right before bed. Maybe I'd be lucky enough to experience all of that in my sleep.

The phone vibrated once, shaking me out of my wishful state. Adam.

Not yet. Should be soon. How are the kids?

Fine. Missing you.

Sorry honey. I hate having to leave you and the kids so much.

I know. But that will be over soon when you leave the firm, right?

No texts came through for a few minutes.

I love you. Got to get to sleep. It's after eleven here.

I noticed he hadn't answered my question about leaving the firm. He always said he missed us, but sometimes I wondered if he secretly enjoyed his trips away from the chaos at home. I flipped my phone back over and shuffled through the rest of the mail. That was about as much communication as I'd gotten out of him in the last week. An official-looking envelope stood out from the junk mail. I peered at it closer. Snowton County District Court. Why were we getting something from the county? I slid my finger along the seal to break it and pulled out the letter.

After scanning through it, I broke out in laughter. Adam had been issued a traffic ticket for running a red light. He always gave me a bad time about my driving, so although I wasn't happy to pay for the ticket, it was nice to have proof that his driving wasn't perfect either.

Upon closer examination, my laughter faded. He'd been issued a ticket on Grand Avenue, a part of Snowton County that he didn't usually have any reason to visit. And the traffic violation occurred midday on a weekday. Why was he there when he should have been in Seattle at work?

I sat back in my chair, idly tracing the edge of the notice

with the tip of my thumb. I'd always thought of Adam as being extremely honest, but now I had some doubts. I checked the calendar on my phone for the date of the incident. I was pretty sure Adam hadn't mentioned leaving work early that day. If the red light camera hadn't caught him, I'd never have known he wasn't at work that afternoon. I flung the notice back on the pile of mail, ironically, on top of the brochure for the Jamaican couples resort.

The lovers on the front stared at me and shook me out of my suspicion. What was I thinking? Was I really considering that my husband was cheating on me? As I discovered more and more about Louis Mahoney, my faith in mankind was diminishing.

It was silly. I knew my husband wasn't cheating on me, and I couldn't believe the idea had crossed my mind. I tacked the notice on the bulletin board so Adam would see it when he got home and finished sorting through the rest of the mail. Most of it was junk that I dumped in the recycle bin.

I spent the rest of the night curled up on the couch with Goldie, watching television. He may not have been Adam, but he was comforting, and that was something I was desperately in need of at the moment.

11

By the next morning, I'd calmed down a little but was still a mess. I was supposed to be at the Boathouse by nine thirty, but I called Beth and told her I'd be in by eleven. After I dropped Mikey off at school, Ella and I walked down to the BeansTalk Café for a much-needed visit with Desi.

Desi was ringing up a customer at the cash register, but she smiled and waved to us when we came in. I busied myself with reading the *Ericksville Times* while I waited. The newspaper staff had managed to get a quote from Terri for their article about the investigation into Louis Mahoney's murder on the front page of the Thursday weekly edition. The byline was that of Niely MacDonald, whom I'd had a run-in with earlier in the year. It wouldn't have been easy getting a quote out of Terri. After dealing with both women myself, I wasn't sure whom I felt more sorry for; Niely or Terri. Niely had noted that there were suspects, but she didn't give any names.

I hastily flipped to the second page. I'd lived through finding Louis's body, and it didn't appear that they had uncovered anything new on the case. However, the article did include information about his funeral, which was scheduled for today at one o'clock. Should I go to it? I hadn't known him when he was alive, so the idea of attending his funeral felt strange. But it would be a good opportunity to casually meet Sandy, Louis's widow.

"Hey." Desi ruffled Ella's hair, causing her niece to smile. "What's up? I thought you'd be heading in to work by now."

"Do you have time to talk?" I asked quietly.

"Yeah, sure." She glanced over at her assistant, who nodded that she'd seen Desi leave. "Let's go sit outside, ok? I need to get some fresh air."

She grabbed cups of coffee for us and led me out a private side door to a small wrought iron bistro table for two.

"When did you put this in?"

"Last week. I found a used patio table and chairs online and bought them to create my own private oasis." She smiled at me. "Sometimes I just want to get away from all the customers on my break. I told my staff they could use it too."

"It's nice." I admired the area. She'd planted colorful flowers in two large white urn planters and hung a bird feeder from the eaves. White lattice fencing enclosed two sides of the patio area, and the café building made a third side, leaving only the view to the water open. It was like being in a secret garden. I liked how it was cheerful, yet distinctly Desi's own style, something I noted for a future upgrade to my office.

"So what's going on? You sounded upset." She picked up her mug of coffee and held it in her hands.

I adjusted Ella in her front carrier and covered her head with a thin blanket. Desi's break spot was mainly shaded by the building, but some sun still broke through. I knew if any sunlight hit Ella's eyes, she'd scream like a vampire caught in a ray of light. "It's a little of everything. Things were going great until we found the body, and now it seems like everything is collapsing around me."

"How so?"

"I'm finding things out about my friends that I didn't want to know."

"About Brenda you mean?"

"Yeah." I was quiet for a moment, watching a bluebird perched on top of the lattice. "Desi—she lied to me about not knowing Louis was allergic to peanuts. She asked me to get cinnamon out of her spice cabinet when I was over at her house, and there was a bottle of peanut extract there. We got to talking about it, and she became nervous and finally admitted that she did know about his allergy."

"So she could have been the one to kill him," Desi said slowly.

"Yes, but I don't think she did." I ran my thumb over the smooth porcelain handle of the mug. "Remember how the basket on Louis's desk had a bow on it? Brenda's don't have that. She uses some sort of heat-seal on them. Whoever opened it to tamper with the chocolates must have tied the top with a ribbon so it didn't look like it had been opened. Also, what motive did she have? She didn't know he was married."

"Maybe she did."

I looked up sharply. "Why would you say that?"

Desi fidgeted in her chair. "When I picked Anthony up at preschool yesterday, I overheard some moms gossiping in the lobby. They were talking about how one of them saw Brenda in her van crying last Wednesday morning. When she got out of her car, the other mom asked her what was wrong." She stared out at the glassy waters of Puget Sound. "Brenda said she had found something out about her boyfriend."

"Wednesday morning. So she knew about Louis's wife before he was killed." I curled over Ella and rested my elbows on the table to cradle my head. My temples had started to throb.

"Yeah. It seems so."

"Crud. That's not good."

We sat in silence, the only sound the crying of seagulls as they flew overhead.

"Do you really think she could have killed him?" I asked. I didn't want to believe Brenda could be a killer and felt guilty even thinking that was possible.

She sighed. "I don't know. You know as well as I do that she was pretty mad at her ex-husband when he cheated on her. I'd hate to see what she'd do if she found out she was the other woman in a relationship."

I tugged at my hair. "This is so messed up. You know, we received a parking ticket notification in the mail yesterday. It was for a part of town that Adam doesn't even have business in from the middle of the day."

"Ok, so what?" She squinted at me.

"So my first thought was to wonder if he was cheating on me."

"Jill." She gave me an incredulous look. "Other than Tomàs, my brother is the most honest man I've ever met. When we were kids, he'd always spill the beans to our parents when we did something wrong."

"I know, I know," I said. "That's how crazy this is making me. Before this happened, the thought would never have crossed my mind that Adam was cheating on me."

"And he's not," she interjected.

"Ok, I know that. My point is that I've been trying to help Brenda out by attempting to figure out who killed Louis, and it's making me nuts. With that weird phone call from my mom, the auction, and everything else, it's just too much. I want to help her, but I can't go on like this." I looked down at Ella and my stomach twisted. I knew what I'd said was true, but I hated the idea of Brenda's husband moving her kids out of state.

"You do have a lot on your plate." She sipped her coffee. "I really want to help Brenda too. I asked Tomàs if he knew anything that might help her, but he said he couldn't talk about the case. He also warned me not to get involved, especially after what happened to you last time you tried to investigate a murder on your own."

"Yeah. That's what I was thinking too. Please don't do anything you aren't comfortable with, Desi. It's just not worth it. And I don't want to cause any problems between you and Tomàs."

"Don't even worry about it. Is there anything I can do to help you with anything else?"

"No, I'm fine. This storm will pass soon." My mind couldn't get away from Brenda's situation. My gut was telling me that she wasn't a murderer. But how could I prove that?

"Brenda wasn't the only woman he was having an affair with. What about Terri?"

She laughed. "You're like a dog with a bone. Is Terri the receptionist you told me about?"

"Yeah." A plane's engine roared high above us, and I waited for the noise to dissipate before I finished my thought. "She didn't seem too pleased that Louis was dating Brenda. And she quit right after he died. She also had access to both the basket from Brenda and to his office."

"But there's nothing linking her to his murder, right? A

basket with chocolates that have been tampered with is pretty damning."

"I know, but that's weird, right? To quit so soon after he was killed? Maybe she's fleeing the country."

"I think you've been watching too many made-for-TV movies. Did his wife know about the affairs? If Tomàs had an affair, I'd be mad enough to kill him."

"Not that I know of. According to his business partner, Dorinda, his wife Sandy was very devoted, always brought him lunch every day. The only bad thing she had to say about her was that she spent money like it was water."

"So if she killed her husband, that would be the end of the cash cow."

"Something like that." A thought occurred to me. "But Dorinda said the business wasn't doing well because Louis had taken so much money out of it, trying to appease his wife."

"So he was single-handedly dragging the business down." She peered into my face. "What would happen to his business partner's investment if Ericksville Espresso failed?"

I leaned back in my chair. I hadn't thought too much about that—or maybe hadn't wanted to consider it. "Dorinda invested her late husband's life insurance proceeds into the business. It means everything to her and her son's future."

"So that would be a huge motive to kill him. Get rid of the guy who was dragging the investment down the tubes and save yourself."

"That's a stretch. Going from losing money to murder is a big leap." Desi did have a point though. I'd become fond of Dorinda and I felt bad for her, but was that coloring my opinion of her? Besides, having a spouse or lover cheating on you was the motive I was hanging on the other women involved in this. Was that a better reason to kill someone?

She laughed. "For what it's worth, Brenda is lucky to call you a friend. With you in her corner, I'm sure everything will work out fine."

Ella stirred in her carrier and I stood. "I hope you're right. I'd better get to work now, but I appreciate the coffee and chat."

"No problem. That's what I'm here for," she said. "Hey, are you going to Louis Mahoney's funeral this afternoon?"

"I hadn't thought about it. Do you think we should? I didn't know the guy well, but I feel like it might be nice since we found his body and all."

"That's what I was thinking too. Do you want to meet me here at twelve thirty and we can go together? Tomàs is home, so I can have him pick up the boys and watch the babies while we're gone."

I checked my work schedule on my phone. I had the last-minute wedding to deal with early in the evening, but the funeral shouldn't interfere with preparations for that. "Sure. I'll see you then."

We walked back into the café's side door, and she returned to working behind the counter, seamlessly picking up a drink order that her assistant called out.

The baby and I walked the few blocks to the Boathouse. Being out in the sun and fresh air had helped my mindset considerably, and even though the pool of possible suspects had opened up, I knew I couldn't give up on my friend.

I met Desi at twelve thirty and drove to the Ericksville Cemetery. A large crowd had gathered around a tent-covered gravesite. For all his faults, as a local business owner, Louis had been well-known in the community. A woman who I presumed to be his wife sat with two college-aged kids in some folding chairs at the front. I couldn't see the woman very well, but I hoped I'd catch a better glimpse of Sandy later.

Desi and I stood at the back of the crowd, unsure of how we fit into the mix. The sky was a bright blue, and the temperature hovered in the low seventies. It was a beautiful day to be outside, and I was sorry to be spending it at a funeral, although I supposed it was better than being stuck in my office at the Boathouse. Beth had generously agreed to watch Ella and Lina in her office so we could attend the funeral.

Desi elbowed me in the side. "Hey."

"Ow. What?" I rubbed the now sore spot on my rib cage.

"Nancy's here."

"Where?" I searched the crowd.

She pointed. "Over there near the front."

I followed her finger and saw Nancy and her husband walking near the open tent. It made sense that she would be here as the deceased was her brother-in-law, but it still felt odd seeing her out of the school setting. It was like finding out your elementary school teacher had a real life other than teaching your class.

Nancy approached Sandy and gave her a hug. Sandy hugged her back stiffly, like you would with a casual acquaintance. I didn't hold it against Sandy—in fact, it made me feel a connection to her. Nancy was a hard person to like. After Nancy left, another woman took her place to comfort Sandy, her long jet-black hair a sharp contrast to Sandy's blonde bob.

The minister rested his hands on the podium and cleared his throat into the microphone. The attendees quieted and the mood became solemn. He read from the Bible and said a few words about Louis. Then he asked for Sandy to come to the front.

She wiped at her tears with a white handkerchief and stood at the podium, staring out at the crowd. Her face was lined with grief as she spoke about her husband. Next, her children talked about their father. All spoke about Louis in glowing terms, as if he had been the best father and husband in the world. I wondered how much of that was true behind closed doors. I'd found people often put on a public front that was completely different than their private life. I assumed Sandy knew of Louis's adultery because of Nancy's nasty comments about Brenda, but did their children know? Or anyone else? As far as I knew, Brenda's name had been kept out of the press thus far.

After the casket had been lowered into the grave, the crowd dispersed. Most people walked back to their cars, but some stuck around to comfort the widow. The teenage children were escorted to a waiting black limousine while their mother stayed at the grave site. Desi started to walk away, but I hooked her arm with mine.

"I'd like to talk with Sandy," I said quietly.

"Really?" She raised an eyebrow. "You don't know her, do you?"

"No, but I'd like to give her my condolences. It seems like the right thing to do, given the circumstances."

She seemed unsure but shrugged. "Ok. Let's go up there."

We waited for the widow to finish talking with everyone else and then walked up to her. She looked startled to see us but stuck out her hand.

"I'm not sure we've met before. Did you know my husband through work?"

"No. I'm Jill Andrews, and this is my sister-in-law, Desi Torres." I wasn't sure how to tell her that we'd been the ones to find her husband's body, but Desi beat me to it.

"We were the ones to discover your husband that day. We're so sorry for your loss."

Her face filled with a mixture of hope and concern. "You found Louis? How did he look? Oh, I hope he wasn't in pain when he died."

Desi and I exchanged glances. Probably not the best time to tell her about her husband's swollen face.

"I don't think he suffered," I said gently. The wind blew a sickly sweet floral odor toward us from a nearby flower arrangement, causing me to stifle a sneeze.

Sandy didn't notice and sobbed into her handkerchief. "I'm glad to hear you say that. I've wanted to speak with you, but I didn't know how to get in touch. Thank you for coming to the service."

"Of course." Desi patted her arm. "Is there something we can get for you? Maybe a cup of water? I think I saw a table with cups on it earlier."

"No, I'm fine, thank you." Her eyes had a far-off look in them. "I told him to keep an EpiPen with him. His allergy was so severe that simply touching anything with peanuts on it could cause him to go into anaphylactic shock."

"I thought he kept an EpiPen in his desk drawer?" I blurted out.

Desi elbowed me again. "Jill," she hissed.

"I'm sorry, I shouldn't have brought it up. It's just I'd heard he kept one in there. When we found him, it looked like he'd been searching for it."

Tears sprung to Sandy's eyes. "He wasn't great about keeping EpiPens with him. He used to keep one in his desk drawer, but after the last one expired a couple of months ago, he didn't replace it." She blew her nose on the white monogrammed cloth, which had Louis's initials on it. "He always told me not to worry, that he wasn't going to eat anything with peanuts in it. He refused to bring an EpiPen with him when we went out to dinner. I always carried one in my purse, just in case. I wish I'd been there for him. I can't believe he's gone." A fresh torrent of tears rained down on her cheeks.

"We're so sorry for your loss." I felt helpless watching her cry.

"If there's anything we can do, please let us know," Desi said. "We spoke with Dorinda and told her the same thing. We feel awful about this."

At the mention of Dorinda, Sandy scoffed. Desi honed in on that.

"I take it things were a little rocky with Dorinda? It's hard to get used to a new partner in a business."

Sandy grimaced. "Taking on a business partner was the worst decision Louis ever made. Ericksville Espresso was doing great until she came along. That woman will drive it into the ground."

I stared at her. Dorinda had said the same thing about her.

"As soon as Louis's estate is settled, I plan to buy out her share of the business." She smiled weakly through her tears. "I'm going to keep Louis's legacy running."

I was still at loss for words, but Desi recovered before me. "Do you plan—"

The minister appeared behind Sandy and put his hand on her arm. "Sandy, we're ready to leave."

She dabbed at her eyes and turned to us. "It was wonderful to meet you both. Thank you for coming." She took his arm and walked away, toward the waiting black limousine.

Desi and I watched her go.

"That was weird." My eyes were still on Sandy as she allowed the minister to help her into the long car.

"Yeah, no kidding."

We turned toward each other. Her eyes were as confused as mine.

"What were you going to ask her?"

"Oh, I was going to ask if she planned to keep Terri on." Her eyes danced mischievously.

"I assume she knew about Brenda, but I wonder if she knew Louis was cheating on her with Terri too? She seems pretty broken up over his death." I didn't know what to believe anymore. Dorinda's account of the finances of Ericksville Espresso contradicted Sandy's. Who to believe— the murdered man's wife, or his new business partner?

Whatever the answer was, something was amiss and someone was lying.

On the way home, I couldn't stop tapping my fingers on the steering wheel. At a stoplight, Desi said, "You're going to wear a hole in that thing."

I wrapped my fingers around the wheel to keep from moving them. The textured plastic grounded me with its familiarity. "I can't help it. I don't want to believe Dorinda had anything to do with Louis's murder."

In the short time I'd known Dorinda, I'd come to like her. With her husband's premature death, the lives of her and her son had been torn apart, and I was rooting for them to regain a sense of normalcy in Ericksville.

"I don't either, but Sandy seemed devoted to her husband. Something isn't adding up."

I didn't answer. When I dropped her off at the BeansTalk, she waved goodbye, and I headed in to work, lost in thought. Having one of my friends as a suspect had been bad, but now I had doubts about both Brenda and Dorinda. I was pretty sure that neither of them had it in them to murder someone, but I'd been surprised before, and I didn't want to let my concerns about them and their children cloud my judgment. I barely knew Terri or Sandy, and it was easier to think ill of them, right or wrong. One thing I did know is that I wasn't sure how I was going to get any work done that day.

As I'd feared, work went slowly the rest of the day. I couldn't focus on anything, and things kept going wrong with the last-minute wedding. By the time I needed to pick up Mikey from preschool, I still wasn't finished with my priority tasks, so we returned to the Boathouse afterward. Lincoln had promised to watch the kids after he finished his work that day, so I would be free for the wedding, but until he was ready, I had both kids.

Having a three-year-old bouncing in and out of my office didn't make work easy, but I'd almost finished when Desi came into the Boathouse with Anthony in tow.

Mikey's eyes lit up when he saw his cousin. "Anthony!" he shouted. Anthony ran to him, and the two of them took off for parts unknown. The front doors were locked and they spent enough time in the Boathouse to know where they were allowed to be, so I didn't worry.

"Sheesh. You'd think it had been years since they saw each other and not hours," Desi observed. She sat down in the uncomfortably padded metal chair I kept in my office for clients. I added buying a nice client chair to my list of office furniture requests.

"No kidding." I tapped out a final e-mail and then closed the lid on my laptop. "What's up?"

"So, I was thinking ..."

I groaned. Nothing good could come of that. I loved being friends with my sister-in-law, but the problem was that we were both too curious about things. We had to take turns bringing the other one down to reality.

"What?" She gave me a wide-eyed look of innocence.

"Ok, ok. What were you thinking?" I knew I'd probably regret asking, but I bit anyway.

"I was thinking," she continued, "we should bring Sandy something to eat, maybe a casserole. I'm sure she doesn't feel up to cooking in this difficult time."

"That's awfully nice of you, but we barely know her." Desi was up to something, but I wasn't sure what it was yet.

"I know, but maybe if we have a chance to talk with her

again, we could figure out whether she or Dorinda is telling the truth." She stared directly into my face. "Don't you want to know? I could tell how upset you were earlier."

My face crumpled as all the energy I'd put into keeping myself from thinking about the situation drained from my body. I slumped in my chair and stared at the ceiling.

"I'm not sure I want to know," I muttered. "Besides, didn't Tomàs warn you to stay out of it? I don't want to upset him. And the police will probably figure out what happened soon."

She waved her hand in the air. "Eh. We're bringing her something to eat, not holding her at knifepoint to interrogate her. What harm can come of bringing a recent widow a nourishing meal?"

She said all that with a straight face. Impressive.

"Desi, you know that's not the reason you want to go. You just want to snoop around."

"Well, we have to find out. For Brenda's sake. I don't want her to lose her kids because she was unknowingly caught up in something completely unrelated to her. We know something isn't right between Sandy and Dorinda. Let's figure out what's going on, and maybe it will clear Brenda."

I sighed. "Fine, but you're making the casserole." I enjoyed cooking, but I knew with the auction items I still needed to clear off my to-do list that evening, I wouldn't have time to make anything. My kids were probably getting microwaved Swedish meatball TV dinners to eat that night.

"Of course." Desi smiled brightly at me. "So you'll come with me? We could go tomorrow afternoon before preschool pick-up. I can get my assistant to watch the café for me."

I scanned my desk. Things were mostly caught up, and I could probably afford to take off an hour or so the next day.

"Fine. I'll do it."

She beamed at me and took off down the hallway, calling Anthony's name as she walked away.

Lincoln showed up soon after she left to take the kids off my hands. I hadn't anticipated the conversation with Desi, and it put me behind in my preparations for the wedding. I knew the catering order had come in, but I hadn't heard anything about the doves yet.

Someone knocked on my door.

"Come in."

Joe, one of our regular waiters, appeared in my doorway. "Hi. There's a man here with some birds."

"Thanks. I'll come out to talk to him." We hadn't worked with this particular provider in the past, so I crossed my fingers that we weren't getting gray carrier pigeons instead of doves.

A man stood in the lobby, shifting his weight. He carried a beautiful gilded cage containing two snow-white doves.

I approached him. "They're gorgeous. Thank you so much for delivering them."

He grinned at me and handed me the cage. "No problem. We're happy to help with the last minute request. Please keep us in mind for future events."

I smiled back at him. "I will. Thanks again."

He turned and walked off, leaving me holding the birds in the cage. They twittered nervously, pacing around on the bar across the cage. I placed them securely in a room where no one would let them out.

The ceremony went off without a hitch, and the bride was ecstatically happy with the venue. Before they left on a brief honeymoon, I handed them the bird cage to release the doves.

The newly married couple gazed into each other's eyes, looking so thrilled to be married that it renewed my hope for true love and marriage. Together, they opened the cage door and the pair of doves fluttered upward.

Everyone followed their progress as they headed out toward Puget Sound. Then a door slammed shut behind someone carrying wedding gifts, and one of the doves was startled. It changed course abruptly, aiming straight for the large window in the Boathouse attic.

The bride's eyes grew wide, and I sucked in my breath. A smashed bird would be disastrous for the event, and a bad omen for the happy couple's marriage. But there was nothing we could do.

Just as suddenly, the bird changed direction, narrowly missing the glass window, and flew out to sea to join its mate. The wedding guests gave a collective sigh of relief, and the groom hugged his bride, pointing at the bird. They waved goodbye to everyone, and I ushered them out the front door to a vintage Ford decorated with tin cans and a large "Newly Married" sign.

When everyone had left, I breathed my own sigh of relief. Although it had seemed like the wedding would end with a sour note, everything had turned out fine—almost to the point of being a textbook perfect wedding. Perhaps that would be a good omen for my future as well.

"Why do I feel like I'm in a spy movie?" I smashed my face closer to the glass, trying to see inside. Desi and I were peering into a front window at Sandy's house after ringing the doorbell. "I don't think she's here."

"You're being silly. We're not spying. We're simply making sure she isn't here before we leave the casserole on her front doorstep. After all, a stray dog could get into the food, and then she wouldn't have dinner. You wouldn't want that, would you?" She somehow managed to say it all without giggling.

I rolled my eyes at her. "I doubt she's in danger of starving. I'm sure she has friends and other relatives who have brought her food."

"But I spent an hour on this lasagna. I want to make sure she gets it. Oh, and by the way, if Tomàs asks, giving a grieving widow a casserole is the only reason we're here. He found me putting it in the oven, and I had to tell him I was taking it to Sandy. He was rather disappointed that we weren't going to be eating it for dinner and seemed suspicious about our intentions." Desi knocked on the door again. Nobody answered.

I had an eerie flashback to knocking on Louis Mahoney's office door and what I'd found in there. I stared at the door.

"What if she's dead in there?" My imagination was working overtime, and I didn't like where it was going.

"Seriously?" Desi balanced the lasagna on one hand and cupped her hand over her eyes, pressing her face to the window again. "The lights are off, and I don't see anyone in there. I don't think she's lying dead on the floor."

"Maybe we should check to make sure." I bit my lip and stared at the door.

"How? I'm sure the door is locked." She turned the knob for emphasis, but the door didn't give.

"Maybe a back door?" I walked toward the side of the house and spotted one on the garage.

Desi followed me, gripping the lasagna pan tightly. I turned the knob on the garage side door and it opened easily. With any luck, the door to the inside of the house wouldn't be locked either.

"We're in." I pushed the door open, unsure of what I'd find in the garage.

Luckily, there was no body in the garage, but it was as cold as a morgue. It looked like this was Sandy's workshop for a florist business. A refrigerated case held cut flowers in clear plastic vases and flower stems and ribbon were strewn across a rough wooden table. Another, much cleaner, table held ornate bows, ready to be wrapped around floral arrangements. I walked to the refrigerator and took a closer look at the formally arranged flowers. The composition was beautiful. Sandy had talent. I spotted a mousetrap in the corner and shivered. More than anything in the world, I hated mice. I'd almost rather discover another body than come across a mouse.

"Sandy?" I called out, my voice echoing off the cement floor and empty walls of the garage. Desi went around me and opened the door into the house. We stood on the threshold, exchanging glances. Entering someone's house felt like more of a violation of privacy than going in their unlocked garage. "Should we go in?"

"We're concerned about her, right?" A pit formed in my stomach, as if we were entering another realm.

"I guess." She stepped into the house, and I followed.

The house itself was much warmer than the garage. Sandy's body wasn't visible, and I breathed a sigh of relief. I wasn't sure if I'd expected to actually find her dead, but I was happy that the house was empty, especially since we were now trespassing for no reason.

Desi made a quick tour of the ranch-style home, her footsteps echoing on the hardwood floors as she disappeared down the long hallway. She returned and set the lasagna pan on the counter.

"I don't think anyone's home." She gestured to the food. "Should I leave this here or take it outside?"

"Outside. I don't want her to know we came in." Now that my fear of finding a body was unfounded, I allowed myself to assess the house. The furnishings were as fancy as Louis's office. The chef's kitchen contained a double oven, a gas stove, and an overhead rack that held an assortment of expensive copper pots. A thick oriental rug covered the hardwood floors in the living room. Above a marble fireplace hung a giant television. "Someone spent a lot of money on this place."

"No kidding." Desi walked over to an antique roll-top

desk situated against the wall next to the kitchen and lifted some papers.

"Desi! You can't go through their stuff." If we messed up her papers, Sandy would know for sure that someone had been inside her house.

"I wanted to see this." She held up a thin manila envelope.

"What is it?" I crossed the thick rug to her, my feet sinking into the plush fibers with every step.

"The return address is a private investigation firm in Seattle."

Our eyes met.

"Is it sealed?" I really hoped not. What was Sandy doing with an envelope from a local PI firm?

"Nope. It's been opened." Desi stuck her hand in the envelope and pulled out a handful of five-by-seven photographs. She flipped them around until they were right side up.

I sucked in my breath. Each photo showed Louis with a different woman—each in a compromising position.

"She knew," I whispered.

"Looks like it." Desi looked closer at the first photo. "There's one with him and Terri. And this one shows him and Brenda kissing." She slid the third photo on top and lifted it closer to her face. I hoped it wasn't Louis with Dorinda, although at this point, very little would surprise me. "I think I know this woman."

"Dorinda?" I crossed my fingers, hoping I was wrong.

"No. Someone who comes into the café. She's married to some high-tech hotshot. I know because she brings it up in every conversation I have with her." She stabbed her finger at the photo. "I always think of her as the gold digger because she never passes up a chance to tell me how wealthy her husband is."

"How did he manage to juggle all these women at the same time? And his wife didn't know." I leaned in to take a closer look at the third woman, a petite woman with dark hair and flawless tan skin. She looked vaguely familiar, although I couldn't place her.

"Maybe she did know the whole time and just wanted proof." Desi shrugged. "What we do know is she knew about this at least since"—she examined the postmark on the envelope— "Monday, June 4th."

"The day before her husband was killed."

"So the question is, was she mad enough to kill him?"

We both realized at the same time that we were standing in the middle of the house of a woman who may have killed her husband. Someone who wouldn't be happy to find out that we'd broken in and rifled through her belongings.

"Put it back," I urged. Desi stuffed the photos back into the manila envelope and artfully arranged it under some papers on the desk, hopefully exactly how she'd found it. She turned to leave and accidentally brushed against another envelope, causing the whole stack to crash to the ground.

I stared at it in horror. "Desi!"

"Oh, crud." She scooped up the papers, holding them in her hands and staring at the mess. "How am I going to figure out what order these were in originally?"

"I don't know, but you'd better do it fast. She might be back any minute." I cast frantic glances at the front door, expecting Sandy to burst through it at any time.

Desi piled the papers on the desk, making sure the manila envelope from the PI was in the middle.

She stood back and examined it with a critical eye. "Does that look about right?"

"I have no clue," I answered truthfully. I wished we'd never gone inside the house, or at the very least, that Desi hadn't snooped through the desk.

"Well, it's going to have to do." She carefully backed away from the desk, and we scurried out of the house through the garage door. In the car, we stared at each other.

"Now what?" I asked. Our list of suspects kept growing. At this rate, there was no way Brenda would get to keep her kids.

"I don't know." Desi rested her head on the steering wheel. "Maybe we should have taken Tomàs's advice and stayed out of it."

I looked out the window at Sandy's front door. I felt as though we'd forgotten something. My stomach dropped to my shoes, and my eyes zeroed in on Desi. Her lap was empty.

"Where's the lasagna?"

"Oh, crap." Desi's eyes bugged out. "In our hurry to get out of there, I must have left it on the counter."

We both got out of the car. "You have to go get it," I urged.

She took off to the side of the garage. When she was out of sight, I heard gravel crunch in the long driveway. Someone was coming. "Desi!" I shouted.

No one answered. She must have already been in the house. What was I going to do when Sandy arrived?

A black BMW pulled into the driveway. A woman's leg appeared out the driver's side, followed quickly by the rest of her. Sandy was home. Desi needed to get out of the house ASAP.

I tried to lean nonchalantly against the side of Desi's car and waved at her. Sandy gave me an odd look.

"Jill, right?"

I nodded and checked for Desi out of the corners of my eyes. Where was she? I was going to have to stall.

"What are you doing here?" Sandy looked around the driveway. She went around to the back of her car and popped the trunk. It was full of paper bags and more florist supplies.

"Uh, my sister-in-law and I wanted to bring you some lasagna. She's a really great cook."

"Oh." She still looked confused. "That's nice of you. But where is it? And where is she?"

I didn't have a great answer for that as I truly didn't know.

"I think she saw an animal or something go around back. Desi's an animal lover and loves to see them in their natural habitat."

Sandy opened her mouth as if to speak, but I cut her off before she could get the words out. "Here, let me help you with those groceries." I approached the trunk of the car and grabbed one of the paper sacks.

"Thanks," she said with surprise. "I didn't expect for anyone to be here. Would you like to come in for a cup of coffee?" She peered at the side of the house. "And your friend too?"

I carried one of the paper sacks of groceries to the front door. "No, we wouldn't want to trouble you. After Desi gets back with the lasagna, we both need to get back to work."

"Oh, ok." She sounded sad. I picked up another bag from the car.

"Last one," I said. She shut the trunk. This bag was quite

full and, as I set it down on the porch, a jar of peanut butter rolled out. I shot Sandy a quizzical look.

"I love peanut butter, but never had the opportunity to buy it when Louis was alive. He wouldn't allow me to have any peanut products in the house. Now that he's gone ..." She inhaled sharply, as if just remembering that her husband wasn't coming home.

"Sandy, we brought something for you." Desi appeared from around the corner, carrying the pan of lasagna.

I let out the breath I'd been holding. That had been way too close.

"Why were you behind the house?" Sandy craned her head around to see where Desi had been.

Desi waved her hand in the air and pointed. "Oh, I saw a bunny hopping off into the woods there. I just love bunnies and wanted to see it closer." She smiled at Sandy and gushed, "You must just love living out here in the country."

"Not really. This was more of Louis's thing. He spent all day at work and wanted to come home and relax away from people." Sandy stared at her house. "Honestly, I'm not sure I'm going to keep the house now." She sighed dramatically. "There're too many memories of Louis here."

I nodded. "I can understand that." I myself wanted to get out of there. Turning to Desi, I said, "We should probably get going."

Desi shoved the tray of lasagna at Sandy, who smiled gratefully at her.

"That was so nice of you. I asked your friend if you could come in for coffee, but she said you had to get going."

"Yes, unfortunately, we've got to get back to work. The instructions for the lasagna are printed on the top." Desi gestured to a white label atop the foil pan. "The pan is disposable, so don't worry about getting it back to me."

"Well, thank you again." Sandy held the lasagna with one hand and unlocked the door with the other. "People have been so good to me since Louis died." Tears appeared in her eyes.

We nodded and waved to her before getting into the car.

As we drove off down the driveway, gravel spitting behind us, I slumped in my seat. "That was way too close."

"No kidding." Desi pushed her foot down on the accelerator as soon as we hit the blacktop. "What were you two talking about?"

"Nothing really. I was trying to make conversation while you were gone. What took you so long anyway? She wanted to know where you were, and I had to tell her you'd gone off to look at some animal. Thank goodness you told her the same story or our excuse for being there would have been toast."

"Sorry. They had their garbage cans right outside the garage, so I stopped to peek at them."

"And you found a big bottle of peanut extract, right?" I was joking, but part of me hoped that was true.

"Sadly, no. The garbage cans were empty. They must have been collected recently." She pulled up to the stoplight at the gateway to Ericksville. From here, I could see all the way to the water and was able to make out the blue roof of the Boathouse. I was still a little creeped out by our trip to Sandy's house and the further we got away from there, the better.

"Great, so even though we now know Sandy knew about Louis's infidelities, we don't know if it was she or Dorinda who was telling the truth about the business." I looked out the window, noticing how beautiful this area was.

"Their house is awfully nice. Those furnishings weren't cheap."

"I know, but maybe Ericksville Espresso used to be really profitable. Or maybe one of them had family money. Just because they have nice stuff doesn't mean they were embezzling from the company."

We were still back at square one. Every new piece of information we found added to the complexity of the puzzle. I hoped we'd find the corner piece soon and could break the case, for Brenda's sake—and mine.

14

By the day before the auction, I'd turned into a harried mess. Two of my friends were on my list of murder suspects, Tomàs was suspicious that Desi and I were investigating Louis's murder, and at the moment, I was nervous about seeing my parents. I couldn't get it out of my head that something was terribly wrong. They'd been in town since last night, but we'd made plans to meet at ten that morning.

After getting the kids buckled in, I got into the minivan, but it seemingly drove on autopilot all the way to the hotel. My parents always stayed with us when they were in town. What was going on? By the time I arrived at the hotel, I'd worked myself into a tizzy, convinced that my mom was dying of cancer or that my father had a different fatal disease. Nothing could have prepared me for truth.

I pulled into a space in the hotel's parking lot and shut off the engine, peering up at the second floor. My stomach twisted painfully. I was used to worrying about my kids, but this was different. These were the people who had been there for me all my life. Psyching myself up with a deep breath, I helped the kids out of the car and walked with them through the automatic sliding doors into the hotel.

When I knocked on the door to their room, my mother answered, looking quite healthy. *So it was my dad who was sick.*

"Where's Dad?" She sighed, and I feared the worst.

"He's next door." Mikey ran to her, hugging her legs.

"What do you mean next door? Why isn't he in here?" I handed Ella to my mom and pushed past her into the hotel room. There was a single king-sized bed in front of a flat screen television. The luggage racks held only one suitcase. The bathroom door was open, but my father wasn't there, or in the main room. Through a connecting door on one side of the room, my father's voice called out, "Are they here?"

"Yes," my mother answered. I heard the sound of the Disney Channel being turned on.

He came through the door looking in better shape than I'd ever seen him. They'd both retired from their teaching jobs at the end of the last school year and now were enjoying retirement. But if they were healthy, what was it they wanted to tell me?

"Mikey, go in the other room. I think Grandpa turned the TV on for you." I pointed at the open door and my father nodded.

"Honey—" my mom began.

"Sweetie—" said my father at the same time.

I looked from one of them to the other. "What is going on?"

Mom snuggled Ella to her chest and took a deep breath. "Your father and I have separated."

"As in you're getting a divorce?" My tone had risen to the Minnie Mouse squeak I always developed when I was highly stressed.

"No, no." My father put his hand on my arm, but I backed away. "Not getting divorced at this time. It's just that we've reached a new time in our lives, and we're taking some time to evaluate whether we want to stay married."

"So you are getting divorced." I sat down on the bed and held my head in my hands. This was the icing on the cake. If I didn't crack up after this week, I could make it through anything.

"No. Like your father said, this is a trial separation," my mother said. She sat down next to me and put her arm around me. I melted into her like a small child needing to be comforted.

"But you're staying in separate rooms," I said slowly. "How long has this been going on?"

They looked at each other guiltily. "A few months. We wanted to tell you in person."

"But you love each other." I felt like someone had taken a baseball bat to my stomach.

My mother nodded. "We do, but we got married so young, and then we had you and your sister. Then we were always busy with work, but now we have a chance to reassess what we want."

"Like what?" I wiped tears from my cheek with the back of my hand.

"Like your father wants us to buy a cabin in Northern Idaho to spend every summer in."

"And your mother wants to tour Europe in luxury instead."

"Ok. So can't you do both?" I looked back and forth between them.

My dad leaned against a wall and stared at the ground.

My mother pressed her lips together and looked at me

with eyes bright with tears. "It's not so much the travel, but that we've realized we're two very different people."

"Ok." I stood, pacing the ground.

As much as I didn't want to, I understood. Although Adam and I had met in college, we hadn't married until we'd both graduated and been out in the workplace for a few years. In that time, we'd both been able to experience the world.

"Does Becky know?" I asked.

"We haven't told her yet," my mother said. "We've been trying to figure out a good time to get down to Oregon to see her." She smoothed a strand of hair away from my face. Her fingers brushed my cheek, sending a pang of longing for my childhood through me.

"Please don't say anything to Becky. We want to be the ones to tell her. We'll let you know as soon as possible if anything changes in our relationship." My father stood in front of me, looking helpless.

I summoned up all the strength I had left. "Can you watch the kids for a few minutes? I'd like to be alone to think about this."

"Sure, honey. Take all the time you need." Mom rocked Ella back and forth.

When I neared the door and was far enough away from them that I thought I could speak without crying, I said in a strained voice, "Thank you for telling me. I do understand, but it's going to take me a while to wrap my head around this."

Their heads bobbed up and down rapidly.

"I love you." I swiveled and escaped to the parking lot, where I sat on a curb, staring blindly at a flowerbed filled with petunias.

My childhood had been pretty close to idyllic. With my

parents both being teachers, we'd spent summers and school breaks camping and playing together. It had always been my sister, me, and them. If my parents divorced, what would holidays with my family look like? Would my parents still celebrate important events together? Would they remarry? Would I like their new partners? I shook my head. I couldn't go down this rabbit hole. I didn't even know what the next week would bring, much less the next few years. For all I knew, they could decide in a few months that they were actually meant for each other.

I dried my eyes and returned to their hotel room. We decided that my father would take Mikey to visit the local children's museum in Everton. Dad was especially eager to teach Mikey about the extensive collection of model trains there, a passion of his. My mother asked if Ella and I would join her for lunch at Lindstrom's before she took my daughter on a shopping spree. I figured dealing with them one-on-one would be preferable to seeing them together, so I agreed.

After helping my father install Mikey's car seat into his SUV, I waved goodbye to my son, made sure my father was prepared for an afternoon with a three-year-old, and left for the mall. Mikey was so excited to see his grandfather that he barely acknowledged I'd left. Neither my mom nor I spoke about the separation the entire way to the mall. When we got there, I dropped her off in front of Lindstrom's, where she was going to return a sweater. Then, I drove around the parking lot until I found a spot that wasn't halfway to the next city, put Ella in her stroller, and speed-walked through the mall, slowing as I approached Lindstrom's. I was nervous about spending time alone with my mom after the bombshell she and my father had dropped on me only an hour earlier.

Ella giggled and I looked up. My mother was walking toward us, making faces at her granddaughter. She'd changed into a knee-length dress that accentuated her svelte figure. I hoped I would look half as good as her when I was in my fifties. I pressed my lips together and swallowed nervously before smiling at her.

"Hey, Mom." I wrapped an arm around her shoulders, and she leaned in. Her familiar Chanel No. 5 perfume encircled me in its comforting embrace. Childhood memories of my family happy together flooded my mind.

"Hey, sweetie." She looked into my face and frowned. "I didn't get a chance to ask you earlier, but are you ok? You have dark circles under your eyes. Have you been sleeping?"

I rubbed my right eye as though I could brush away the dark bags under them which had appeared a week ago.

"Let's check out the makeup counter at Lindstrom's after lunch, ok?"

"Sure, Mom." I knew the only thing that would truly help was for the auction to be over, for Louis's murderer to be found, and for my parents to kiss and make up. That, and about one hundred hours straight of sleep.

"You know, you need to take better care of yourself." She looked me up and down. "Have you been eating right and exercising?"

"Mom." I fought to keep my tone in check. "When am I supposed to exercise? I have two little kids and a busy life. Right now, exercise isn't top of my priorities."

"Well it should be. You need to take care of yourself now, so you'll feel your best later in life. Your father and I go to the gym several times a week." She eyed me. "Have you been eating vegetables and whole grains?"

I felt like a child being reprimanded by their parent for not eating their broccoli at dinner. My blood pressure rose.

"I do the best I can." Did french fries count as a vegetable? I figured that was a stretch. As a long-time physical education and health teacher, Mom had made a career out of exercising and eating healthy. Somehow, I hadn't inherited her zest for it. She was right though, I did need to take better care of myself. Maybe then I wouldn't be so tired all the time.

She wrestled Ella's stroller out of my grip and walked purposefully toward the department store, not stopping until we reached the elevator. I followed dutifully behind them, wishing I was back in my office working on the auction preparations rather than hanging out in a department store during work hours.

"You like Lindy's Café, right? You always did when you were a kid." Worry clouded her eyes.

"I do like it." I smiled at her. "Thanks for thinking of it, Mom." Could it be that she was just as nervous around me as I was with her?

I did love Lindy's Café. While the store itself was pretentious and employed haughty salespeople, the café was decorated in a style that I called atrium-chic. It was filled with plants and sunlight, and they piped bird noises through speakers. I felt as though I'd been transported into a jungle paradise. The food itself was varied, and I'd never disliked anything I ever ordered there. It had been awhile since I'd gone there though. With two kids, a household, and a job, I had very little time to hang out with friends on a leisurely day at the mall. I missed that. My botched girls' night out with Desi had been the closest I'd come in a long time to having fun with a friend without the kids around. Being a mom was great, but sometimes I missed my independence.

After we'd ordered, my mom played peek-a-boo with Ella, who was propped up in a high chair between us. Ella soon tired of the game and occupied herself with picking Cheerios off the table instead. After she'd scattered all the cereal, she focused on a stuffed parrot hanging in nearby tree.

"So how have things been going?" my mother asked. The waitress set our drinks on the table and scurried away.

"Stressful. You know we have Mikey's school auction tomorrow night, but in addition to that, Desi and I found an auction donor's body last week when we went to his office to pick up a donation. Everything since then has been a mess." I sipped my Diet Coke.

"Oh, honey, I'm sorry. That's horrible. Did you know the man?"

"No, but one of my friends did, and now she's one of the police's main suspects."

She raised her eyebrows. "He was murdered? Your friend killed him?"

"No," I said, in a sharper tone than I'd intended. "I mean, yes he was murdered, but I don't think she did it. But she was dating him, and he turned out to be married, which she didn't know."

"Did his wife know about her?"

"Yes, it appears that she did." I wasn't going to tell her how Desi and I had discovered that little nugget of information. I didn't want that to get back to Tomàs. He had already seen through our decision to bring Sandy food, and he didn't need to know we'd broken into her house as well.

"So maybe she killed him." She looked pleased at her deduction.

I smiled. "Maybe, but she seemed devastated by his death. By all accounts, she was devoted to him." The peanut butter she'd bought still struck me as odd. It was almost a jab at her dead husband to buy it immediately after he was put in the ground.

"Well, women can do funny things when their trust is broken." She frowned. "A friend of mine—"

Suddenly, I had the feeling of ice running through my veins. "Mom," I whispered.

She looked up. "What is it?"

"Did Dad ... cheat on you?"

A smile crept across her face. "No, of course not. Your father would never do that. How could you ever think that?"

I breathed a sigh of relief. "Then why did things not work out between you two?"

Her smile faded, and she reached out for my hand. "Honey, as I told you before, we just want to take a break from each other. You have to understand, we're different people than we were when we got married. It wasn't as apparent when we were both working, but now that we're retired, we're stumbling over each other in the house."

"Is Dad moving out? Are you?" I couldn't imagine my childhood home without both of them in it.

"Your father has moved to the bedroom in the basement while we sort all of this out." She smiled. "He's got quite a little bachelor kitchen there, with a mini-fridge, microwave, and toaster oven."

I stared at her. It sounded awful, although my dad had never been much of a cook, so it was probably good enough for his toast and TV dinners. I didn't know what to say.

"Ok." I removed my silverware from the paper napkin and placed it on my lap.

"Anyway, I didn't have a chance to finish telling you about my friend. Usually, she's quite mild-mannered; the stereotypical meek librarian, but when she discovered her husband was cheating on her, she went a little crazy. She threw all of his clothes out their bedroom window and set fire to them on the lawn. Then she slashed all of his tires. Finally, she emptied the bank accounts and went on a month-long cruise. He didn't know what hit him."

"Wow. She was really mad." Mom's friend must have been in a lot of pain, not that I blamed her.

"Yeah, no kidding. When people are hurt, they lash out in ways that you wouldn't expect."

That made sense. —In Louis's case, every one of the suspects had reason to be hurt; some by relationship infidelity and some by financial infidelity. Any one of the people Desi and I had considered suspects could have murdered him. It all made my head hurt, and the dissolution of my parents' marriage didn't help.

The waitress put our plates of food in front of us. I'd ordered a mozzarella and tomato panini with a side salad, which my mother gave a look of approval. She dug into her fava bean salad and that was the end of our conversation about their marriage. Perhaps it was for the best. Although their marriage affected me, how they wanted to spend their future really was up to them.

Twenty minutes later, we'd both devoured our food. After paying the bill, Mom looked up at me. "Did you still want to come with me to the makeup counter? I think some of the Clinical Face's under eye cream would make a big difference. With all your work on the auction, you want to make sure you look your best tomorrow."

"Sure." She had a point. I didn't want to look like death warmed over at the auction.

We got off the elevator on the first floor, and I pushed Ella toward the giant cosmetics section in the middle of the store. The collision of scents from hundreds of different perfumes assaulted me as we grew closer to the center mass.

Mom pointed to a counter off to the side. "There's the Clinical Face counter."

When we reached Clinical Face, a woman with dark hair and a white lab coat was brushing blush onto a woman's face. With her back to us, the salesperson held up a mirror for the woman in the chair to see. Apparently the customer was pleased with her reflection because she smiled and nodded at the salesperson, who selected a box from a shelf and deposited it in a small paper bag. After paying, the woman left the store with a spring in her step. Without turning around, the salesperson busied herself with organizing the remaining products on the shelf.

My mother cleared her throat to alert her to our presence. The woman in the white lab coat spun around, her hair swinging around her like a glossy black cape.

When she'd completed her revolution, my eyes widened. It was the woman that the PI had photographed with Louis. And, I realized, the same woman that I'd seen with Sandy at the funeral. A perky white name tag on her smock read *Macy*.

"Hi," she said in a cheery tone. "How can I help you today? Would you like to try our new firming lotion?" She didn't give any indication that she'd recognized me, not that I expected she would.

"Not today, thanks. My daughter is interested in trying your eye cream." Mom pointed at my face. "She's been under a lot of stress lately."

The salesperson motioned for me to sit in the chair, but my feet refused to budge. My mother nudged me toward the chair, pressing on my shoulders until I sat. She gave me an odd look, probably wondering why I was so distant. I couldn't help it, though—my mind raced with uncertainty. Should I say something to the salesperson? Let her know that I'd seen the photos of her with Louis? That I knew she was sleeping with her friend's husband?

"Ah, stress lines and lack of sleep, I know how to cheat that." The dark-haired woman snapped her fingers. "We'll use the eye cream and the skin perfecter."

I let her work her magic, my thoughts stuck on her statement that she knew how to cheat. My mother looked on, cheering me with words of encouragement. "You look so much better, honey. Doesn't Mommy look good, Ella?"

Ella let out a shriek, which turned into a crying and screaming jag. Mom tried to rock the stroller back and forth to soothe her, but the baby wasn't having any of it and continued to wail.

I pushed the salesperson's hand aside to address her. "She's getting tired. It's probably time for a nap." I looked up at the woman holding a brush an inch away from my eye. "I'm almost done, right?"

Macy picked up the mirror she'd used earlier and showed me my reflection. One eye glowed, rejuvenated by the voodoo magic in their cream; the other was still sallow and dejected. "A couple more minutes, ok?"

I swallowed. "Sure. Mom, can you take Ella outside? She might do better with some fresh air."

She nodded and redirected Ella's stroller toward the side entrance. "Meet us out there when you're done, ok?"

"She's got quite a set of lungs on her," Macy observed before returning to my face.

I looked into her eyes, not sure if this was my chance or not. Then, I remembered my half-finished face. If I wanted to make it out of the store without strange looks from the other customers, I should probably wait for her to complete the transformation.

When she finished, she handed me the mirror. While admiring her handiwork, which admittedly took five years off my real age, I tried to gently pry information out of her.

"You know, you look really familiar." I pretended to be trying to place her. "Didn't I see you at Louis Mahoney's funeral?"

She turned away from me, but I could see her face flush in the mirrored back counter of the Clinical Face booth. Bottles clinked gently against each other as she rearranged items on the shelves, avoiding my question.

"It was so awful about him dying," I said. She still hadn't moved. "Did you know him well?"

Finally, she faced me. "My husband and I have been friends with Louis and Sandy for years. Yes, it was a horrible thing to happen."

Nothing Macy said seemed suspicious in the least, other than the fact that I'd seen proof she was cheating with her friend's husband. That probably wouldn't have gone over well with either her husband or Sandy.

"My condolences to you and your husband."

"How did you know Louis?" she asked politely.

"Oh. My sister-in-law and I were the ones who found him after his death."

"Oh my. I didn't know." She rubbed her fingers along the plump edge of a blush brush. "How awful for you."

"It was." I went in for the kill. "Even worse for my friend Brenda, who was dating him. I mean, I don't want to speak ill of the dead, but she had no idea he was married. I feel so bad for her."

She grimaced. "Louis wasn't exactly a faithful husband."

"No, he wasn't, was he?" I stared directly into her eyes.

She squirmed and narrowed her eyes at me. "You know about me and Louis, don't you?"

I nodded.

"How do you know?" she whispered. "We were so careful."

"Someone I know had pictures."

"Pictures?" She blanched so white that her carefully applied blush and contouring powder gave her the appearance of a circus clown. Macy leaned against the counter and stared at the floor before gazing back up at me. "Do you think Sandy knows?"

"Do *you* think she knows about you two?"

She picked up a tube of eyeliner and twisted it between her fingers. "I don't think so, but I don't know for sure." She stared at me with heavily mascaraed eyes. "You aren't going to tell her, are you?"

I tilted my head back but didn't say anything else. The tinny announcer's voice came over the loudspeaker, advising Risa to answer line ninety-nine. When it finished, Macy spoke again, her eyes full of pain.

"I never meant to hurt her, but there was something so irresistible about him."

I'd never met Louis while he was alive, but from what little I knew of him, I had a hard time reconciling his looks and personality with the description of him being irresistible. Then again, he'd managed to snare Brenda and she was usually a hard sell. There must have been a quality to him that was indiscernible after death.

"Did your husband know about you and Louis?"

She hung her head. "Yes. He found out two weeks ago and moved out of the house."

"Do you think he could have been involved with Louis's death?" The other women that Louis had dated recently had all been single. A married woman's husband wouldn't have taken kindly to his wife cheating with one of their friends. And, as someone who'd known Louis for a while, he most likely knew about his peanut allergy.

"No, no. He'd never have done anything like that," she said. "If he were going to mess with Louis, it would be more along the lines of hacking into his bank accounts. Besides, he never knew who it was, only that I'd had an affair."

"Do you know where he was when Louis was killed?"

"Yeah. He's been in Hong Kong for the last two weeks, ever since he moved out. His company is doing business there. I'm telling you, it wasn't him."

A woman hovered near the edges of the cosmetics counter. She plucked packages off the counter in between glances at Macy.

Macy smiled at the woman and held up a finger to signal she'd be with her in a minute. "Look, I can't talk with you all day about this. Now that my husband is out of the picture, I have to make money. Do you want this or not?" She held up the container of eye cream.

I checked my reflection. Macy had worked miracles on my face. If this cream was half as good when I applied it at home, it was worth whatever she was charging for it.

"Sure." I paid her the forty dollars for the cream and walked away from the counter. When I got close to the edges of the cosmetics area, I turned back to look at her. She was talking animatedly with the new customer.

Ella and my Mom were waiting outside for me on a bench. Mom held Ella in her arms, with her feet touching her legs.

"She's walking already." Mom grinned.

"Haha. Thank goodness she isn't really. I'm not ready for that yet. One mobile child is enough for now."

"You look great, honey."

"Thanks." It was amazing how the small act of putting makeup on made me feel so much better. I might even do it more often if I had time. "Do you still want to hang out with Ella for the rest of the afternoon?"

She placed Ella back in her stroller. "Oh yes, we're going to head off to the children's area here. I saw the cutest ducky pajamas there when we walked past."

"Ok, well, she'll probably fall asleep in the stroller soon. Give me call when you're ready for me to pick you up. I can give you a ride back to the hotel so Dad doesn't have to." I waved to Ella as she rolled past me.

"Sounds good," she called over her shoulder.

Alone with my thoughts in the car, I couldn't help but dwell on Louis's murder again. The PI had only taken pictures of three women, but there could have been more. Then again, juggling those three plus a wife and business would have taken all of his time. Someone close to him had most likely killed him.

15

The night of the auction came all too fast. I'd gone over my lists several times to make sure everything was on track, but butterflies still fluttered in my stomach. The setup crew had situated the tables according to the seating chart, and the catering staff was in the process of covering them with red tablecloths, silverware, and glasses.

The doors to the Boathouse's main room were open to view the deck outside. I'd hung a banner over the door that read "Busy Bees Auction". The maintenance staff had hosed down the deck to remove any trace of seagulls and had swept it clean. This was going to be the best auction the school had ever seen.

I allowed myself a moment to lean against the deck railing and stare out at the water, the wind blowing my hair behind me. I'd taken Goldie with me to work that day because he'd been antsy at home with me gone so much, and he was running up and down the dock, excitedly barking at the seagulls flying overhead. I'd have to either lock him up in my office or take him home before the auction started. A fisherman in an aluminum boat passed by and waved at me. I smiled and waved back at him.

I turned back to the Boathouse and admired the building. When Beth and Lincoln had rescued the aging boathouse left over from Ericksville's days as a fishing resort, they'd repainted it white and left the blue roof on it. The baby blue color was an iconic part of Ericksville's downtown now.

"Jill," Beth shouted from behind me. "Someone's on the phone for you."

I nodded and followed her back inside the building.

In my office, I picked up the phone. "Jill speaking."

"It's Nancy. How is everything with the auction? You aren't answering your cell phone. Do you need me to come early to manage things?"

I counted to ten. She always had to micromanage everything. "No, Nancy. We're fine. I've got everything under control." I'd purposefully ignored all of her calls to my cell.

"I'll be there an hour early to make sure everything is perfect." She hung up.

I stared at the phone. *Soon this will all be over.*

A few hours later, I returned from taking Goldie home to find Nancy directing my staff in the main room.

"What are you doing?" I looked at her with incredulity.

"Making sure they are doing this right. I don't know how you let them get away with such sloppiness. I mean, the forks need to be a lot closer to the plates for a proper place setting. And the buffet table—the dressing tureen should be at the end with the other condiments, not with the salad."

Behind her, the catering crew cowered in a corner. I approached them. "It looks great, guys." They nodded in relief and scurried out of the room. I turned my attention to Nancy. "This is my staff. Guests aren't allowed in here for another hour. Kindly leave until we are open." Ice dripped from my words.

Her mouth gaped open like a fish. "Well. If you want to run things in such a slipshod fashion, go right ahead. But we won't be holding any more events here in the future." She spun on her heel and huffed out of the room.

A smile slid across my face as I watched her retreat. I hoped she meant what she said about not having any future auctions at the Boathouse. Someone clapped from the side entrance, and I spun around to see who had witnessed our interaction.

"Oh goodness, thank you," Beth said, a wide smile spreading across her face. "I've been wanting to get rid of that woman since she arrived, but it was your project, and I didn't want to intrude."

"Unfortunately, she'll be back in an hour with the rest of the guests." I frowned. With any luck, Nancy would be in a better mood when she was in her element as the head Queen Bee at the event.

After dealing with Nancy, I retreated to my office. The dress I'd bought to wear to the auction hung on the back of the door. I locked the door and changed into it. My first pair of pantyhose had a run in them, but I'd planned for that and brought a spare. I slipped on silver kitten heels over the new pair of stockings and exited the room to check my appearance in the bathroom mirror. I'd bought the dress a month ago but hadn't tried it on since wearing it in the store. *Please let it still fit,* I thought. I smoothed down the blue chiffon skirt and gazed at my reflection. It fit me like a glove. My face flushed with happiness. Maybe it was a sign that the auction would go off without a hitch.

By a quarter to the hour that the guests would arrive, we'd placed the miniature airplanes at each table as centerpieces and hung pictures of historic planes on the walls. Above the auctioneer's podium hung a child-sized ride-on plane that one of the parents, a flight aficionado, had donated.

Desi came in with Tomàs in tow and hugged me. "You've done a great job."

"Thanks." It felt good to hear someone say that after all the work I'd put into the auction. I looked around the room, taking it in the way a guest would. It did look wonderful. The decorations were perfectly arranged and not overdone, creating an elegant effect. In spite of Nancy, I'd done well.

"You look gorgeous." She wore a short violet dress and looked like a million bucks.

"Why, thank you." She preened and then complimented my dress.

I smiled and pointed at the plane hanging from the ceiling. "Wouldn't the boys love that?"

She stared up at the toy airplane. "Anthony would die if we brought that home, but it would take up half his bedroom. I think we'll stick to bidding on something a little smaller."

I laughed. "My thoughts exactly. But some little boy or girl will be very happy to get it."

Desi and Tomàs had volunteered to staff the booth at the front door to provide information and drink tickets to the guests, so I showed them where the silent auction portion would be. Then, I left for that room to check on setup. The other members of the auction committee had arranged the silent auction items artfully on tables covered with white tablecloths. At the far end of the room, they'd hung a few art pieces that were available to bid on. The Ericksville Espresso basket held a prominent position at the end of one of the long tables. Just seeing the artful bow on the top made me shiver.

The guests started to arrive, and I circulated throughout the event center to ensure everything was going well. Nancy came in with a sour expression on her face, holding on to her husband's arm tightly. His pinched face made it obvious that he'd rather be anywhere else, whether due to the recent loss of his brother-in-law or because he disliked school auctions, I didn't know. As soon as Nancy saw some of the other Queen Bees, she ditched her husband and he took off for the bar. I made myself as invisible as possible and jetted to the other side of the room, away from Nancy. I knew that I'd have to talk with her at some point, but I planned to put that off for as long as possible.

Brenda came in, wearing a sleeveless cocktail dress, trimmed with silver beads. Her skin was sallow, and the dress was loose on her. She glanced around the room nervously. "Is Nancy here yet?"

"Yeah." I pointed at the swarm of Queen Bees. "She's over there."

"Good, then I'm going this way." She smiled at me and then wandered off in the opposite direction of Nancy.

Dorinda entered soon after Brenda. She hugged me. "It's beautiful, and I love this building. I'd seen it from afar, but I've never been inside until now."

"Thanks. My in-laws have worked hard on the building." I beamed with pride at her compliments. "I'd better keep moving. If something goes wrong, Nancy will be on me faster than I can blink."

"Good idea. Hey, is that airplane up for auction?" She pointed at the hanging plane that Desi and I had discussed earlier.

"It is. Do you think Daniel would like it?"

She nodded. "He'd love it. He's really into planes, just like his father." Her face fell at the mention of her deceased husband.

"Well, then you should definitely bid on it." I squeezed her shoulder. "The bar's over there if you want anything."

She smiled faintly and said "thanks" before walking toward the bar.

One of the auction committee members announced that bidding for the silent auction items had commenced, and the attendees flooded the smaller room. As they milled around the tables, the guests chatted amongst themselves, already lubricated for social interaction by one or two adult beverages. Some of the parents I hardly recognized as I usually saw them wearing "just woke up" attire, rather than cocktail finery.

I checked my watch. It was already ten after six, and Adam hadn't yet shown up. He'd promised to be there for the auction, and I hadn't heard from him since his plane landed over two hours ago. As if on cue, he entered the door to the smaller event space. He wore a black suit and blue tie, and my heart swelled with joy at seeing him for the first time in over a week. He smiled at me, and I melted a little.

"Hey," he said, leaning down and kissing me on the check. "Sorry I was late. The traffic from the airport was horrible, and then I had to stop off at home to change."

"Hey. I'm glad you're here. I was starting to worry you weren't going to make it." It wouldn't have been the first time work had made him miss a date with me.

He closed his eyes for a moment and sighed, looking contrite. "I'm sorry I was late. But I know the auction is important, and that you've worked hard on it. Nothing was going to keep me away." He stepped back and looked me up and down. "You look great. Is that a new dress?"

"It is." I twirled around to show him the pleats in my royal-blue chiffon dress. "You look great yourself." I knew he was making an effort with me, and I stood on my tiptoes to kiss him. "Did you see the kids at all when you were home?"

"I did." He laughed. "Your father was on all fours, and Mikey was pretending to ride him like a horse."

I smiled at the image. My father had let my sister and I play horsey with him when we were kids too. Some things never changed. "How was Ella?"

"She was in the high chair. Your mom was giving her pears." He rubbed my shoulders. "Don't worry, honey. The kids are fine."

"I'm not so much worried about the kids, but about how my parents are doing."

"They're doing great, why?" He gave me a funny look and I realized I hadn't told him about yet about my parents' separation. I didn't really want to get into that at the auction, so I didn't say anything about it.

"Hey, is there anything good to bid on?" He scanned the tables from where we stood.

I shrugged. "Probably. I haven't had much time to look. Do you want to check things out and place some bids for us? We should probably bid on something. It is for Mikey's school."

"Sure, honey." He pecked my cheek again and strode off to review the first silent auction item.

I spun around slowly, trying to take in the whole room. With satisfaction, I noted that all of the guests were talking and laughing. A warmth rose up in me, and a smile spread across my face. I'd made this happen. Everything appeared fine, so I left the room to check the other event spaces.

Beth came out of her office as I walked past and gave me

a thumbs-up. "I'm heading home to help Lincoln with Desi's kids. How are your parents doing with Mikey and Ella?"

"Adam was just at home and said they're doing fine. I've been so wrapped up in this that I haven't even checked my phone." I pulled the phone out of my small evening purse. No messages. "Looks like everything is ok."

"Good." She hugged me. "I'm so proud of you, Jill. This is great. I couldn't have done better myself."

I beamed with pride. "Thanks, Beth. That means a lot to me. I'm really starting to like working here." Juggling a career along with the taking care of the mounds of dirty laundry, dishes, and everything else that came with having a family wasn't easy, but I knew I'd made the right decision to work at the Boathouse.

She smiled. "I'm glad to hear that. I knew you would. Lincoln and I are just a call away if you need anything, ok?"

I gave her a little wave. "Have a nice evening."

She left. I had an odd moment where I felt very alone, but it quickly passed. There was too much on the agenda for me to have time to doubt my abilities at this late date.

I rounded the corner in the hallway to the front lobby. Loud voices drew me to the other hallway, closer to my office. I peeked my head around to see what was going on. Nancy had cornered Brenda in the hallway and was shaking her finger at her.

"You just had to go after him, didn't you?" Nancy had her back to me, so I couldn't see her expression, but I was willing to bet her face was bright red with anger.

Caged in against the wall, Brenda held an empty wine glass by her side. "You don't know what you're talking about."

"My husband's family is a mess now. His sister can barely function, and my niece and nephew are devastated."

"I'm sorry for their loss." Brenda tried to placate her, but her words had little effect. I wasn't sure whether I should intervene or not.

"What kind of floozy dates a married man?" Nancy's voice slurred with the aftereffects of more than a few cocktails.

Brenda tried to edge away. "Nancy. You have to believe me. I didn't know he was married."

"How could you not?" Nancy cried.

Brenda shook her head and forcefully walked around Nancy, who spun around, ready to follow her. I stepped into the hallway, and Brenda came to stand next to me.

"I think she's had a few too many," she whispered to me then said in a louder voice, "I'm getting so tired of defending myself about Louis. I honestly had no clue he was married, and I certainly didn't kill him. Am I ever going to get away from this?" She sounded close to tears.

I put an arm around her and guided her back down the hallway toward the rest of the guests. "It will get better, I promise. I'm sure the police will figure this out."

"They'd better. If it doesn't happen soon, I'm going to lose my kids." Her brown eyes were devoid of emotion, as if she'd given up. She walked away from me toward the rest of the guests.

I turned back to my arch-nemesis. She'd crumpled to the floor in her orange flowered dress and was crying. I hated seeing anyone in that position, even someone I hated.

"Nancy?" I held out a tissue from my purse. She grabbed it and swiped at her face. "Are you ok?"

"No," she sobbed. "I feel so bad for my sister-in-law. She shouldn't have to go through this."

I handed her another tissue. "I'm sorry. This must be hard on your family."

She stared up at me, as if just now realizing who she had confided in, then pushed herself up and glared at me before stalking away. I wasn't terribly surprised, although a small part of me had hoped there was a nicer side to Nancy than I'd previously experienced.

16

*A*fter the silent auction had closed, the Boathouse event staff and I herded the guests into the main room. As they entered, guests oohed and aahed over the photos of historic flights that we'd placed on the wall. Everyone seemed impressed by the boarding passes with seat assignments and the staff dressed as flight attendants. I puffed up a bit when I overheard one woman say it was the most professionally organized auction she'd ever been to.

At the podium, the auctioneer, a man we'd hired from a local service, cleared his throat and announced that dinner would be served soon. Everyone took their seats. I'd reserved a table on the edge near the front of the room for Desi, Tomàs, Adam, and I. Brenda, Dorinda, and another couple I didn't recognize joined us as well, rounding out our group. We introduced ourselves. The couple I didn't know had a daughter in the two-year-old class and a baby.

When our table was called, I approached the buffet table with some trepidation. I knew it was silly because I'd already confirmed that the full amount of filet mignon had been delivered, but part of me worried that there would be a mix-up because of my ordering error earlier in the week.

Adam put his hand on my shoulder, as if sensing my concern. "It all looks great, honey."

I looked up at him and smiled, before continuing on down the line and filling my plate with beef, mashed potatoes, salad, and a roll. I'd attended many events at the Boathouse before and knew the food would be well received, but I still scanned peoples' faces to see what they thought. A server caught my eye and gave me the thumbs-up sign. I grinned and returned the gesture.

Back at our table, an envelope had appeared.

Dorinda picked it up. "Dessert Dash."

Desi groaned. "I'd hoped they wouldn't do that this year."

"What is it?" I hadn't attended the auction last year and hadn't been involved with this part of the planning this year.

"All of us put money into the envelope. Whichever table donates the most money gets to send their representative to the dessert table first." She pointed to the back of the room at a table overflowing with sweet offerings. All of the men at the table fixated on it.

"So everyone at the table gets the same thing?" I asked. Nobody answered.

"Look at that," the man I didn't know said. "One of the items is orange Jell-O." He and his wife both wrinkled their noses.

Adam looked at me very seriously. "I have to have that chocolate cake. How much do we have to donate?"

I laughed. He was as much of a chocoholic as I was. "I don't know. Probably hundreds of dollars to win first place."

Desi leaned over to her brother and whispered to him loud enough that the rest of the table could hear, "I made that. It's my special truffle cake. Come to my café, and I'll give you a piece. It'll save our table a ton of money."

Adam's expression was hilarious. He kept glancing from his sister to the cake and then back to me with a pathetic pout to his lips.

"Oh, fine," Desi said. "It's for the kids." She forked over a fistful of money and stuffed it in the manila envelope.

"Yeah," said the other man. "I really don't want the Jell-O." He nudged his wife until she dipped into her purse and put some money in the pot. The rest of the table followed suit.

"All right, ladies and gentlemen, time's up." The auctioneer motioned to one of the auction committee members to gather the envelopes.

"Our first item up for auction is a weekend at a beautiful cabin on Lake Eider." He went on to describe the attributes of the cabin and how much fun a family would have there. The bidding got up to eight hundred dollars before someone won it.

"Next, we have this wonderful gift basket for a night out on the town. Tickets to the Seattle Theater for June 23rd and a night at the Hightown Hotel, including dinner at Seabeck's Restaurant in downtown Seattle."

I glanced at Adam. It had been a while since we'd had a date night. I elbowed him in the side.

"Ouch." He rubbed his side. "What was that for?"

"Do you want to bid on it?" I asked, a little too eagerly. "Wouldn't a night out without the kids be great?"

He slid his gaze to the PowerPoint slide with the item's details. "June 23rd."

"Yeah. We're free that night—we should totally go for it." My spirits rose. Our wedding anniversary was on June 24th and after the events of the last few weeks, I deserved a night out. I knew I wasn't going to get a Caribbean vacation, but I'd settle for dinner and theater in Seattle.

"I don't know, honey. I think I'll be out of town that day." His eyes met mine. They sparkled with a hint of something, but I wasn't sure what.

"Oh," I said in a dejected tone. Of course he'd be out of town. I teared up a little, probably from the stress.

He put his hand on mine. "We'll do something else, ok?"

"Uh huh." I nodded but shifted my hand away from his. I wasn't going to put any money on his promise.

The other auction items passed in a blur. Toward the end, the auctioneer pointed at the toy airplane hanging from the ceiling.

"We'll start the bidding on this absolutely amazing child-sized airplane at nine hundred dollars." A slide showing a smiling little boy appeared on the screen. The crowd rustled with interest.

"Are you going to go for it?" I asked Dorinda, who was sitting next to me.

She stared at the airplane. "I don't know. It's awfully expensive, but Daniel would love it."

The auctioneer started the bidding, and Dorinda put her paddle up. Across the room, a woman stood, raising her paddle to bid against her. With a shock, I realized it was Sandy. What was she doing here? And why was she bidding against Dorinda?

Nancy had said her sister-in-law was barely holding it together, so maybe she'd invited her to get her out of the house. However, looking at her now, I wouldn't have described her as distraught. Sandy glared defiantly at Dorinda. The flush in her cheeks was the only color in her face, made even more pale in contrast with her long-sleeved black dress. Her appearance was that of a mourning widow, but her actions were not. Why did she hate Dorinda so much?

"What's that all about?" I asked Dorinda.

"I have no idea." She stared at the other bidder. "I offered to buy out her share of Ericksville Espresso, and she refused. Said she was going to buy me out. I told her 'good luck with that.' It didn't go over well. But to try to win something that I want for my kid? That's a little crazy."

Nancy smirked at us from her seat next to Sandy. Apparently our entire table was hated by them. I smiled pleasantly back at her, and she turned around.

Sandy continued to bid Dorinda up, but Dorinda held on and finally won the airplane for an exorbitant sum.

I caught her eye after her win. "I really hope Daniel likes that."

She laughed. "Me too. But I couldn't let Sandy win. I don't know why she hates me so much, but I didn't want to let her walk all over me."

"And now, we'll pause the live auction for the results of our dessert dash," the auctioneer announced. The crowd murmured in anticipation.

"We'd better not get the Jell-O," Adam said darkly. I sighed and patted his arm.

We didn't win the highest bid and lost out on the truffle cake, but a plate of gourmet pecan brownies appeased Adam.

"Who got stuck with the Jell-O?" Desi asked, scanning the crowd. "Oh." Her eyes danced with mirth.

I twisted in my chair to see who she was looking at. Nancy and Sandy's table had received the orange gelatin dessert. It sat on their plates, untouched. Nancy's arms were crossed over her chest, and the discontented expression on her face was priceless. Their table wasn't full and therefore hadn't had as much opportunity to raise money toward the dessert bid. I averted my gaze and turned back to the table before a broad smile spread across my lips.

The rest of the auction went off without a hitch. As it was winding down, guests paid for their silent and live auction items.

Adam tapped me on the shoulder. "I need to go pay for our silent auction items."

"What did you bid on?" I was curious to find out what he'd chosen. With any luck, it wasn't a year's worth of truffles.

"You'll see." He bopped me on the nose and headed off toward the cashier. One year, he'd given me a kitchen sponge holder in the shape of a frog, and I'm not a big fan of frogs. I wasn't sure I wanted to see what he'd bought now.

Someone bumped into me, and I turned to see who it was.

Nancy glared at me. "Where did you get those filet mignons from? They tasted like shoe leather."

I bit my tongue, literally. It was the only thing I could do to not lash into her.

"We source our meat from local butchers. Everything is grass-fed and organic."

"Well, they tasted horrible." She shook her head. "I knew I should have handled this. If I want something done right, I've got to do it myself."

"I'm sorry you feel that way." My hands curled into balls, and I forced them to open, pressing them against the cool fabric of my dress.

"And as if this event could get worse, that woman dared to show up tonight. After what she did to my sister-in-law and everything. Everything was great before Louis met her. I can't believe she had the nerve to bid against Sandy." Her vehement words carried with them the scent of too many alcoholic drinks.

Nancy must have been drunker than I'd thought if she believed it had been Brenda bidding against Sandy. I hoped she wasn't driving.

"Is your husband around?" I scanned the room but didn't see him.

"He's busy consoling Sandy. You and your friends need to stay away from her. She told me how you were at her house with lasagna. She doesn't need your pity." She huffed at me and spun around, swaying slightly as she walked.

Somehow, Nancy always managed to impress me by bringing me to dislike her even more with every interaction. I'm usually pretty tolerant of other people, but she rubbed me the wrong way, and her hatred of my friends was going too far. However, this was my place of business and, technically, she was a guest. This wasn't the time or place to tell her off, but I hoped that day wasn't too far in the future.

As I watched, her husband and Sandy approached her. He took her arm and led her away toward the Boathouse's lobby. Well, at least she had a designated driver. I turned away, happy that I wouldn't have to deal with Nancy again that evening.

Adam came towards me, his eyes bright. He held something behind his back. What had he bought this time? I didn't have room in my kitchen for another sponge frog.

"Ta-da," he said, revealing the basket he held in his hands.

My eyes bugged out. He'd won the gift basket Brenda had donated, practically a carbon copy of the one from Louis's desk.

"It's chocolate," he said happily. "See, it's even got that chocolate wine you love."

I smiled weakly. My eyes stuck on the box of chocolates at the bottom of the basket, and my stomach lurched. He'd meant well, but I never wanted to see another of those baskets ever again.

"Wow, that looks amazing," I lied. "We'll have to save that for our anniversary."

He grinned proudly. "I knew you'd like it. I'll go put it in the car and then come back to help, ok?"

"Sure, thanks." With any luck, the basket would mysteriously be stolen out of our car before we got home.

The auction guests were trickling out of the Boathouse. I said goodbye to my friends and checked on the staff, who were already cleaning up. Soon, only Desi and Tomàs remained.

"Nice job, Jill," Desi said, hugging me.

"This was so much better than last year. I couldn't even eat that shoe leather they called chicken cordon bleu last year." Tomàs shifted on his feet, holding a gift basket and envelope that they'd won in the silent auction.

"Thanks."

He cleared his throat. "That woman that was bidding against your friend Dorinda ... that was Louis Mahoney's widow, wasn't it?"

Desi fidgeted with her dress and looked down.

"I believe it was," I said. "Dorinda told me they'd argued, and Sandy seems to have it out for her."

He looked at me and then at his wife. "You two aren't asking around about the Mahoney murder, are you?"

I didn't know what to say.

Desi put her hand on his arm. "Sandy is Nancy Davenport's sister-in-law, which is why she's here. Ericksville Espresso donated a gift basket to the auction."

She'd neatly sidestepped Tomàs's question, but I didn't think he'd completely bought it.

"Ok. I know you two are close to this, especially with finding Mahoney's body, but please remember that the police are handling the investigation."

Desi and I nodded solemnly. Luckily for us, Lincoln walked up to us, breaking up our conversation.

"Jill, I've got it from here. Go home, relax. I'll stay until everything is cleaned up. Anthony and Lina are both asleep, so Beth said I could come over here."

"Goodnight, Dad," Desi said, tugging on her husband's arm and leading him out the door.

I was torn between wanting to stay and see the event to completion and wanting to relax on my couch with a huge glass of wine. The wine won out, although it wouldn't be the chocolate wine from the basket. I might be able to drink that again in a few months, but the memories of Louis's death were still too fresh to enjoy it now.

17

I woke up Sunday morning and lay there for a moment staring up at the ceiling. I rolled over to find Adam next to me, snoring softly. Down the hall, Ella cried out, and I eased out of bed, careful not to wake Adam. I picked up Ella and changed her, then crossed the hall to Mikey's room. He was quietly playing with action figures on the rug in his room.

"Hey, I didn't even know you were up." I sat down next to him, laying Ella on her tummy. She pushed herself up and eyed me with disdain for being forced to do tummy-time. Her brother shrugged.

"Nobody else was up."

I hugged him. "Remember what today is?"

He sat up straighter as realization flooded into him. "It's my birthday party!" His eyes sparkled as he jumped up and galloped around the room. "My birthday!"

I held my finger to my lips. "Shh. Daddy's still sleeping."

"Ok," he said, but continued galloping in a circle. "My birthday party, my birthday party!" he whispered loudly. His little sister looked at him like he was crazy.

Smiling, I touched his arm. "Let's go downstairs. I need to start getting things ready, like making your cake."

He ran out of the room and down the stairs before I'd even lifted Ella off the floor. Downstairs, I managed to get them both seated at the dining room table and served them Cheerios and milk. Most of Ella's went on the floor, but I think Mikey ate some while he bounced excitedly.

The Teenage Mutant Ninja Turtle decorations sat on the table, staring up at me like a green glowing reminder that I still had to bake him a cake. Desi usually made his cakes, but with a new baby, I hadn't wanted to impose on her. Mikey had requested a chocolate cake in the shape of a Ninja Turtle. I was no baker, so I hoped it wouldn't look like a pile of muddy grass when I was done. I pulled out a box of cake mix and was staring at it when the front doorbell rang.

Desi stood on my doorstep holding a domed tray. My eyes widened.

"Is that what I think it is?" I really, really hoped it was a birthday cake.

"Yep." She removed the dome top to reveal a perfect representation of Michelangelo the Ninja Turtle. I motioned for her to come in.

"You're a lifesaver. I checked out Pinterest for cake ideas, but they all looked so complicated. This is awesome."

"You're welcome." She smiled then whispered, "Are Nancy and her daughter coming this afternoon?"

"Nope. Unfortunately, she let me know that they had another commitment and wouldn't be able to attend." I wiggled my eyebrows. "Can you tell how sad I am about that?"

Desi laughed.

"Is it chocolate?" Mikey came to the door, bouncing around his aunt.

"It is." She knelt down to his level. "Double chocolate with chocolate chips."

"Yay!" He wrapped his arms around her.

"Happy birthday, buddy." She stood and turned to me. "Anthony's looking forward to the party. Tomàs has to work, but we'll be there at one. I'd better get back home before Lina wakes up again." She waved goodbye and left.

"That cake is so cool," Mikey said, his eyes as big as mine had been when Desi showed up.

"It is," I agreed. I re-covered the cake. "Now, go play. Mommy has a lot to get done."

The cake had been one of the big items on my list, but now that it was no longer an issue, I unfortunately had time to worry about some other things, namely how Daniel would behave around the other kids and what it would be like to hang out with both of my parents together. Neither were something I could control.

By the time Mikey's guests arrived, our house resembled a sewer—a Ninja Turtle sewer, at least. I'd hung green and black streamers from the walls and strategically placed some round "sewer" entrances in the hallway and living room. Mikey, for one, seemed enchanted by it. About half his preschool class had RSVP'd, along with their parents, and both sets of his grandparents.

Dorinda showed up with Daniel in tow about ten minutes after one o'clock. Our family had arrived, but the other guests weren't there yet. Ella was being passed around between her adoring grandparents.

"Go ahead and put your gift on the table over there." I motioned to a table near the fireplace. "Mikey and Anthony are playing upstairs if you'd like to join them," I said to Daniel.

Daniel ran upstairs, and Dorinda grinned at me.

"Thanks, Jill. It means a lot to him to have the other kids accept him."

"No problem." I crossed my fingers that Mikey would behave, and it wouldn't be an issue. "We're glad to have both of you here. C'mon, I'll introduce you to my family."

She followed me into the living room where my parents, Adam's parents, and Desi sat on the couches chatting.

"You know Desi, but these are my parents, Ann and John, and my husband's parents, Lincoln and Beth."

Dorinda flashed them a smile.

"Everyone, this is Dorinda. She and her son Daniel are new in town. She's a part owner of Ericksville Espresso, which is where Desi gets the coffee beans for the café from."

Beth's mouth formed into an O. I could tell her mind was full of questions about the other co-owner of the company, but she recovered smoothly. "Oh, yes, and I believe Desi buys your beans for the Boathouse too. It's nice to meet you, Dorinda."

Someone rang the doorbell, and I left them to answer it. A few of Mikey's friends and their parents stood there, holding out gifts. I smiled at them and led them into the house.

"Mikey, time to come down here!" I shouted up the stairs. It was fine for him to play in his room with a couple of kids, but I didn't want ten kids up there breaking stuff and getting into trouble.

The boys clopped down the stairs. Daniel seemed to be getting along with them well—until he saw the other kids. Then, he became shy, hanging on his mother. When everyone was there, I announced that we'd be playing some games. With Adam's help, we herded the kids over to one hall where I'd pinned a picture of a Ninja Turtle sans mask.

I clapped my hands. "Ok, we're going to blindfold you

and spin you around and have each of you try to pin the mask on the Turtle." I nodded to Adam, who put a bandanna around the first boy's eyes and spun him around. As the boy tottered sideways from dizziness, Adam handed him the mask and pointed him in the right direction. The group cheered as he applied the mask around the turtle's neck.

Daniel went next but grew so dizzy that he bumped into one of the other kids.

"Hey, watch it," the boy said. He pushed Daniel back toward the picture.

Daniel stopped in place and ripped off his blindfold. He glared at the kid who'd pushed him.

"Boys, please don't push your friends," Adam reprimanded.

"He's always running into us on purpose though," the pusher whined.

"It was an accident." Daniel folded his arms over his chest. The whole group backed away from him a few steps.

His mom noticed and rushed over to the group. "Hey, Daniel, why don't you come sit with me for a few minutes."

"Fine. I don't want to be here anyway."

I thought I saw some tears form in the corners of his eyes. It must be difficult to be the new kid in town. "I think it was an accident," I said loudly to the children. All eyes turned to me while Daniel and his mom exited to where the other adults were gathered in the living room and kitchen. "Let's finish up this game, and then I've got something else planned."

The boys grumbled a little but obeyed. I shot a glance at my parents. They sat on couches opposite from each other, each chatting with another adult. I hadn't seen them exhibit any animosity toward each other, but their marital separation still made me nervous about what was to come in the future. I didn't like the idea of not having them together at family events.

We finished up the other game, a balloon toss in the backyard, and then I announced it was time for Mikey to open his presents.

"Yay!" he shouted, running back into the house. His friends trailed behind him, along with the few parents who had gone outside to watch the balloon game. Daniel had stayed inside with his mom.

Mikey opened his presents and was surprisingly polite about everything, even when he received two of the same toy. Afterward, we gathered around the dining room table to sing "Happy Birthday" to him. Dorinda nudged her son to join the other children, who were kneeling around the coffee table eating cake. She sat down next to me on a kitchen stool.

"Whew. Who would have thought a children's party would be a minefield of activities." She scooped up a piece of cake and popped it in her mouth, as if starving for a comforting carbohydrate.

"Sorry." I felt guilty that Daniel wasn't having more fun. The boys seemed wary of him, though, and rightfully so if he'd been antagonistic toward them at school. I shot a glance at the kids. Daniel didn't have a spot around the coffee table, but he sat near them and was laughing about something alongside the other boys. "He seems to be doing ok now."

"I hope so." She put down her fork to stare at her son. "It's been a tough year—for both of us." She sighed. "Buying Ericksville Espresso was supposed to be a new start for us, but now it's like we're being punished. The business is leaking money, and we'll probably lose clients with Louis's death." She looked at her son again. "Things need to start getting better soon."

"I'm sure things will get better. When the police find out who killed Louis, you'll be able to move on with the business, right?"

"I don't know. Sandy Mahoney is making my life miserable. She's convinced the police that I was doing something illegal or inappropriate with the business's finances."

I stared at her. "I thought you said she was taking too much money out of the business."

She pushed uneaten cake across her plate, trailing crumbs behind her fork. "She is, but I'm the new guy in town. She's telling everyone it's me who is killing the business."

I chewed on a bite of cake. The icing tasted overly sweet. Probably more my perception of it than Desi's cake-baking skills. Dorinda was the new person in town and, as much as I liked her and wanted to help her, how did I know she was telling me the truth about the goings-on at Ericksville Espresso?

I stood, dumping my paper cake plate into the garbage can I'd set up in the dining room. I put my hand on Dorinda's shoulder and squeezed it. "I'm sure it will all work out, ok?"

"Thanks, Jill." She picked up her plate and put it in the garbage too, before checking her watch. "Daniel and I had better go. We're supposed to have an early dinner with his grandparents tonight. They're going to take him camping for a few days."

"That sounds fun. I hope he has a good time. Will you still be around?"

"Yeah. Until this whole mess at work is cleared up, I'm

not going anywhere." She frowned slightly. "Thanks so much for the lovely party. I hope Mikey likes his gift."

"I'm sure he will." I smiled at her and watched as she collected her son and her belongings. They were the first of the guests to leave, but the others followed soon afterward.

Before Brenda left with her girls, she pulled me aside. "You didn't say anything to the police about the peanut extract, right?"

"No, of course not. Why do you ask?" I put down the icing-soiled napkins I'd cleared from the table.

"The police were at my house again, asking me more questions about the chocolates." Her face crumpled, and she looked near tears. "Brad has requested an expedited custody hearing because he's thinking about accepting that out-of-state job and moving next month. If that happens, I'm sure it will come up in the court proceedings that I'm suspected of killing Louis Mahoney. What kind of fit mother is a murder suspect?" Tears slid out now, and she swiped furiously at them with the back of her hand.

My head hurt. I'd have thought the police would have solved Louis's murder by now. All I could do was pat her arm and try to console her.

Dara and Sara bopped up to their mom, amped up on sugar from too much cake and ice cream.

"Can we go to the park on the way home?" Sara asked.

"Sure," Brenda said, hugging them close to her body. "And we'll stop by McDonald's afterwards for Happy Meals. Sound good?"

They nodded.

"Thank you for the nice party," she said, her voice artificially cheerful. "The girls enjoyed themselves."

I walked them to the door. "Thank you for the gift and

for coming. And, Brenda, if there's anything I can do, please let me know."

"I will." Her voice caught with emotion, and she rushed the girls to the sidewalk.

My mother stacked up paper plates and cups while my father attempted to sweep up cake crumbs off the table. I stopped them. "You don't have to do that. I'll take care of it. I know you wanted to see your friends this evening."

They exchanged glances. "Are you sure?" Mom asked.

"Of course. Go." I smiled at them, and they reluctantly gathered up their belongings and left.

Soon, only Adam, Mikey, Ella, and I remained.

"It looks like a tornado went through the house," Adam calmly observed.

"No kidding." I liked throwing big birthday parties for Mikey, but I absolutely hated the clean-up. I surveyed the ruins. "Maybe I should have let Mom help." Thinking about my mom brought back the worries I'd had about how her separation from Dad would affect us as a family. They'd seemed happy enough being together in the same room, but what if things turned ugly between them?

"Maybe," he said. "But I think it will be ok." He tilted his head to the side. "Are you feeling ok?"

"I'm fine. Just worrying about my parents."

"They seem good together. Give them time to figure things out."

"I know, but I can't help worrying." I surveyed the mess again. This wouldn't be fun to clean.

"I'll make you a deal," Adam said, coming up behind me and encircling my waist with his arms. "If you make dinner, I'll work on getting this cleaned up."

I turned around and looked into his face. "Seriously? You'll do it all?"

He shrugged. "Yeah, shouldn't take too long."

I had my doubts about that, but I agreed. "Ok, chicken tetrazzini coming right up."

Adam gathered stray paper cups and plates and dumped them in the garbage while I readied the dinner ingredients. When I popped the pan of tetrazzini into the oven an hour later, he was almost done cleaning up. I put on a pot of coffee and perched on the edge of a stool. Ella was taking a nap, and Mikey had retreated to his room to play with his new toys. He was surprisingly trustworthy, but I still checked on him every ten minutes or so to make sure he hadn't gotten into any trouble.

My husband finished cleaning and plopped himself down on the stool next to mine. "How does it get so messy in such a short amount of time?" he asked in wonder.

I shrugged. "Ten little boys and girls and their parents can do that to a place."

"How about we have the party at the pizza place next time?"

I laughed. "Good idea." The coffee finished percolating, and I poured each of us a cup.

I sat back down, and all the adrenaline I'd had over the last few weeks drained out of my body. The auction was done, and we'd made it through Mikey's birthday party. Other than my basic work projects, I didn't have anything else on the horizon.

"Your friend Dorinda seems nice," Adam remarked. "I met her at the auction, but we didn't really have much time to talk until today."

"She is." I still felt uneasy about my doubts about her.

"But?" His eyes drilled into my face, and I squirmed.

"But what?" I sipped my coffee to avoid talking to him.

"You're acting funny about her." He stared at me accusingly. "I thought you were friends?"

"We are." I set the cup down on the counter. "But with all this stuff going on with Ericksville Espresso, I don't know what to think."

"Jill, spill. What's going on?"

I took a deep breath. "After finding Louis's body, I feel like I have a responsibility to figure out what happened there. And I hate that Brenda is their main suspect."

"So? What are you not telling me?"

"Dorinda claims that Louis's wife, Sandy, is taking excessive amounts of money out of the business. But Sandy says it's the other way around—that Dorinda is doing something unethical. I want to believe Dorinda, but what do I really know about her, other than she's the mom of a kid in Mikey's class?"

"True, but you like her, right?"

"I do." I wrapped my fingers around the cup's handle.

"Well, what do you know about Louis's wife?"

"Not much." I understood his point. I didn't really know either woman well although I felt a strong bond with Dorinda. But did that mean Sandy was lying?

Ella cried upstairs, and I pushed myself away from the counter. "Thanks, Adam. I appreciate you trying to help."

"No problem." He put a hand on my arm as I brushed past him. "Honey, I know I'm traveling a lot, but I'm only a phone call away. I want to stay involved in your and the kids' lives. If something's bothering you, I want to know."

I met his gaze, and a smile formed on my lips. "Thanks. I appreciate it." I went upstairs to check on Ella, my mind still spinning. Who was telling the truth, Dorinda or Sandy? And did the inner workings of Ericksville Espresso have anything to do with Louis's murder?

18

_M_y parents had taken Mikey for the day, so I only had Ella with me and was free of preschool pick-up responsibilities for the afternoon. I had to work a half day at the Boathouse and then deliver one of the larger auction items. Dorinda had won the large toy plane and wasn't able to get it home in her car, so I'd told her I would bring it to her in my minivan. If it didn't fit in there, I'd have to borrow Tomàs's truck to transport it.

When I finished work mid-afternoon, I stopped off at the BeansTalk Café to see Desi and grab a cup of coffee before heading over to Dorinda's house.

"Hey." She came over to me and gave me a hug as I approached the counter. It was an off time of day for café business, so it wasn't too crowded in there. "What's with the helmet?" She gestured to the child-size aviator's helmet peeking out of my bag.

"It goes with the plane I'm taking to Dorinda, but I was worried that if I didn't put it somewhere obvious to me, I'd forget it in the car."

"Ah." She nodded. "That makes sense. So the plane fit in your minivan?"

"Yeah, just barely. I had to remove some seats and wedge it in there."

"I'm sure Anthony would have loved it, but that thing is gigantic." She shook her head. "Are you recovered from planning all your own events?"

"Almost." I smiled. She was right. Somehow, my day job as an event planner was much easier than planning personal events like the preschool auction or Mikey's birthday party. I suppose it was because, although I always did my best to exceed client expectations, I didn't have anything emotionally invested in the success of a client's wedding or reunion.

"Thankfully, after I get Dorinda's plane delivered, I'll be free of the Busy Bees Preschool Auction." I nodded toward my car.

She raised an eyebrow. "Yeah, good luck with that. You did such an awesome job this year that Nancy's definitely going to ask you to help again next year."

"There's no way she can talk me into doing it again. One time was enough. Plus, she was full of complaints about the food and about the Boathouse as a venue. I don't think she'll have any interest in having another auction there."

Desi brought two cups of coffee over to a small round table and set them on it, sliding one over to me. I dropped my bag on the floor and carefully set Ella's carrier next to it. Sitting, I sipped the coffee, marveling at how good Ericksville Espresso's beans tasted, even if I couldn't discern the subtle flavor nuances.

She laughed. "Nancy has a way of convincing people to do things they didn't think they wanted to do."

"Well, she's not going to succeed with me."

"She got you to do it in the first place, didn't she?"

Desi had a point. I'd accidentally volunteered to manage the auction at the Boathouse, and it had been Nancy who had orchestrated that. I'd have to steer clear of her next year when auction planning time came around again. Not that avoiding her would be a major inconvenience to me.

"So how is everything else going?" Desi asked.

I shrugged. "It's going."

"How's Brenda? I saw you talking with her yesterday at Mikey's birthday party. I didn't want to butt in, but she looked really upset." She fiddled with her coffee cup. "I hope everything is ok."

"The police questioned her again, and her ex-husband is still threatening to take the kids out-of-state. With Louis's murder unsolved, Brenda's name can't be cleared, and it's not helping her custody case." I slumped back in my chair. I'd tried my best, but there didn't seem to be anything I could do to help my friend. Unless ...

"Has Tomàs said anything more to you about the murder investigation?"

"Not much. He doesn't want us trying to investigate on our own, and he's not allowed to talk about his cases to me in detail, so I've heard even less about this case than usual."

"Do you know if they checked whether Terri, his assistant, has an alibi?"

"He did say that they don't think it was an employee who did it, so I guess that rules out Terri."

"But not Dorinda or Brenda," I said slowly. This wasn't great news.

"Or his wife. The way she was acting at the auction was nuts. I've never seen anyone shoot daggers at another person for so long." Desi was quiet for a moment, then asked tentatively, "What do we really know about Dorinda?"

"Not much." I sipped my coffee, but it was lukewarm and unappealing. "She bought into Ericksville Espresso after her husband died. Her in-laws live in Everton, and she wanted her son to be close to them."

"From what I've heard about Louis over the years, he was rather pompous. I can't imagine he'd sell part of his business unless he really needed to." Desi's eyes followed a customer as he left his empty mug in the dish bin and walked out the door of the café.

"That's the impression I've gotten too. But does that mean Dorinda is telling the truth? That Louis and Sandy were having some financial problems? Or did he just want some extra cash?"

"I don't know. It's not like we can ask Sandy about it. She'd probably bite off our heads."

"Maybe I can get some information out of Dorinda when I bring the airplane to her." I checked the clock on the wall. It was after four. I was supposed to meet my parents for dinner at five thirty, and I still needed to deliver the airplane and pry more details out of Dorinda.

I slung my bag over my shoulder and grabbed Ella's carrier. "I'd better go. Thanks for the coffee and words of wisdom."

"No problem." Desi regarded me. "I'll talk to Tomàs, but I'm not sure I'll get anything else out of him."

"Thanks." I walked to the door and pushed it open, angling Ella's carrier through the opening.

Outside, the sun shone brightly. I set Ella down and put my sunglasses on before proceeding to my car.

I'd left my car windows open to keep the temperature from building up inside. There wasn't much of value in there other than Dorinda's toy plane, and I figured someone would notice if a thief tried to steal it. Actually, seeing someone attempt to steal it would be rather entertaining. I wasn't sure I would be able to free it from my car when I got to Dorinda's house.

I pushed the button to slide the van door open and snapped Ella's carrier into the base in the captain's chair. The entire rest of the van was taken up by the giant red plane. Good thing my parents had Mikey, or I wouldn't have been able to fit it in my vehicle with two car seats in the back. There was no way Dorinda could have fit it into her sedan.

A big red bow encircled the nose of the plane, reminding me of Brenda's gift baskets. Her baskets were heat sealed and whoever had opened the plastic to tamper with the chocolates had tied a bow on top to hide their misdoings. But who? I knew Terri, Dorinda, Sandy, and Brenda had all had access to the basket. I couldn't get the bow out of my mind. A niggling feeling told me it could be the key to this whole puzzle.

19

I pulled up at Dorinda's house and managed to parallel park between two other vehicles along the neat cement curb. She lived in an older part of town, up on the hill, where an alley ran behind the houses. Her house was a charming Victorian that I knew Brenda would love. A small plastic bulldozer sat forlornly in the middle of the front lawn, so I was pretty sure I had the right house.

I needed to move Ella's seat to get the airplane out, so I opened the sliding door of my minivan and released her car seat from the base. I brought her up the front steps, setting her carrier in a far corner of the enclosed porch to allow myself plenty of room to get the airplane up the stairs. I removed my sunglasses to see better on the darker porch and eyed the door. How was it going to get through that door? Maybe if we turned it sideways it would fit. One thing was for sure—I'd need Dorinda's assistance to get the airplane inside. I'd had help from some of the Boathouse staff to load it into my car, and I wasn't sure I could lift it by myself.

I glanced at Ella and smiled. She looked so angelic,

sleeping in her carrier next to a long white planter filled with purple and gold pansies. It was weird to think that next summer she'd be toddling around. With much effort, I pulled my attention away from the adorable baby, back to Dorinda's airplane.

I rang the doorbell, but there was no response. She'd told me she would be there, so I tried knocking instead. Muffled voices filtered through the door, which I now noticed wasn't closed all the way. Dorinda had the same problem with her door not latching completely as I did with our deck door. It swung open under the gentle force of my knock.

I paused on the sensible black doormat. The door was ajar, but I felt weird entering Dorinda's house by myself as I didn't know her very well.

"Hello?" I shouted into the dark room.

A hand reached out and hooked my arm, yanking me out of the bright sunlight into an unusually dark room. Dorinda must have had the best light-blocking drapes that money could buy.

Blinded by the lack of light, I stumbled on a carpet inside the door, but the person kept pulling on my arm, their sharp fingernails digging into my skin. They led me through the room. My thigh banged against an end table and something large on the table, like a lamp, wobbled then settled in place. I rubbed my leg. That was going to leave a bruise.

"Ouch! What are you doing?" I said. What was going on? Why was Dorinda acting like this? The fingernails pressed harder into my skin, and I was thrust onto a soft object near the back wall that I assumed was a couch.

Someone next to me breathed in short puffs of air. The person who'd shoved me down paced in front of me. I willed my eyes to adjust to the dark, but my pupils were still small after being in the bright sun. The tension in the air was so thick you could cut it with a knife. Who was sitting next to me, and who had grabbed me? I heard footsteps on the carpet as my attacker paced the living room.

He or she was still invisible, but I could finally make out the person sitting next to me. "Dorinda?" I whispered.

She nodded. Her hands were tied behind her back, and her feet were bound as well.

"Stop talking," a woman ordered. She came closer.

"Sandy?"

What was Sandy Mahoney doing in Dorinda's house? With the animosity between them, I couldn't imagine they'd been having a friendly afternoon coffee chat.

"Quiet." She continued pacing.

Next to me, Dorinda shook. I placed my hand on her arm, and she calmed a little. My eyes darted across the room. I still didn't understand why she was tied up or why Sandy had essentially kidnapped me, but I assumed it had something to do with Louis's murder.

I tried being nice. "Sandy," I said tentatively. "What's going on? Is there something I can help you with?"

"No, you've helped enough." Her words came out a sharp as knives. "I had a police officer stop by my house today. Apparently someone told them I had hired a private investigator to follow my husband and his floozies. I know it was you and that friend of yours from the Boathouse."

Shoot. How had she found out Desi and I knew about the photos?

As if she'd heard my internal thoughts, she laughed. "Did you really think I wouldn't be suspicious when you were just standing there outside my house? And your friend —looking for a bunny? Really?"

She came closer to me, and I made out the shape of a gun in her right hand. I pushed myself further into the couch cushions, as if that could protect me from her.

"The papers on my desk were out of order, so I knew someone had been in there. It had to have been you two."

"I didn't say anything to the police," I said, not admitting to breaking in. I knew Desi must have told Tomàs about the photos.

"Right," she said sarcastically. "They just showed up on my doorstep for no reason." She waved the gun at us.

I patted my front jeans pocket for my cell phone. It wasn't there. I must have left it in the minivan while I was carrying Ella up to the front porch.

Ella. My heart dropped to my knees, and icy dread took its place in my chest. I'd left Ella outside. Whatever Sandy had planned for Dorinda and I, it wasn't good. I didn't want Ella to be hurt. I'm not very religious, but I sent up a prayer that my baby girl wouldn't wake up and alert Sandy to her presence by crying. I wondered where Daniel was. I hadn't heard anyone else in the home, and I hoped Sandy hadn't hurt him.

"Why are you doing this?" I asked.

"Well, Dorinda wouldn't take my offer to buy out the other shares of Ericksville Espresso."

I shot a glance at Dorinda. My eyes had grown accustomed to the dark and, in the thin stream of light from the window above the front door, I saw the terror on her face. I needed to keep Sandy talking while I thought of some way to get us out of there.

"Why did you want to buy her shares? Why not sell and take the money?"

"Because the business was Louis's dream. I'd already taken some money out of it, but I intended to drain all the money from it and run it into the ground, just like he did with our marriage. Of course, I'd be sure to move that money into a nice safe investment account. After all, I have to look out for my future now that I'm a widow."

I couldn't clearly see her face, but her voice held a self-satisfied tone.

"So you killed him." I now realized why the pretty silk ribbon bows had stuck in my mind. Brenda had said she wasn't crafty, and her baskets had been simple but elegant. Sandy's house had been the one filled with bows, just like the one on the basket from Brenda on Louis's desk.

She shrugged, as if killing her husband was no big deal. "He deserved it. I was fed up with his cheating, but I knew if I divorced him, I'd get nothing. I'm in my mid-forties and my floral business is only for fun. What would I do for money?" She laughed again, a horrible grating noise. I scooted closer to Dorinda and reached behind my back to try to untie her bonds—bonds which I now realized were tied with the same silk ribbon. Sandy really loved that stuff.

"Enough with all this though—I need to get going."

"How did you know I'd be here today?"

"I didn't. I hadn't decided what to do with you yet. But when the doorbell rang and Dorinda told me it was you, I congratulated myself on my good fortune. Two birds with one stone and all." She chuckled, an evil sound that caused another icy finger of fear to poke at my spine.

"What are you going to do to us?" I wasn't sure I wanted to know the answer.

"Oh, you and Dorinda will die in a tragic gas explosion. Two friends visiting when the oven malfunctions and blows up the house." She came over to me and set the gun down on the arm of the couch while she tied up my hands and feet. I contemplated kicking her in the face, then eyed the gun and decided it would be too dangerous to go for it. Next to me, Dorinda trembled.

Sandy stood and picked the gun back up, assessing the two of us. Seemingly satisfied with her efforts to restrain us, she retreated to the kitchen.

When she was out of the room, I immediately turned to Dorinda.

"Where's Daniel?" I asked urgently.

"He's with his grandparents, thank goodness. What are you doing here?" she whispered.

"I was delivering the airplane like we discussed." My pulse settled a little with the realization that Daniel was safe. I'd forgotten she'd told me at Mikey's birthday party that his grandparents were taking him camping. If he'd been in a different room, I didn't know how I'd fit him into whatever escape plan I could concoct.

"Oh yeah. It slipped my mind after I got home from work and Sandy surprised me." She leaned against the arm of the couch.

"Ella's on the porch." My voice wobbled. If Sandy blew up the house, the porch would go up in flames. I had to figure out a way out of there. I twisted my wrists, trying to wriggle out of the bonds.

Dorinda closed her eyes for a moment. When she spoke, her words were tearful. "I'm so sorry I got you into this mess. I had no idea she was so crazy. She showed up on my doorstep this afternoon, claiming she wanted to talk about the business, so I let her in. As soon as I did, she pulled a gun on me."

The odor of natural gas trickled into the room. We didn't have much time. Sandy's footsteps echoed in the kitchen, and she came back into the living room, approaching us.

"I'd say I'm sorry, but I'm really not. With you two out of

the picture, I can plant evidence that Dorinda killed my husband. I'll be the grieving widow, and she'll be the evil co-owner. It works out perfectly."

She looked at me. "You'll be the innocent victim who was caught up in all of this." She sounded strangely happy about the prospect of my death. "I've set a toaster on a timer. When it ignites the gas, I'll already be home."

I shivered. Sandy was truly insane. The ribbon around my wrists stretched a little, and I freed one hand behind my back, then the other. I leaned closer to Dorinda and picked at the ribbon encircling her wrists. They'd been tied too tight to loosen.

Sandy took a final look around the room, then exited out the back door. Something briefly covered the daylight coming from the window above the front door. Was Sandy eliminating our last bit of light to leave us in blinding darkness before the house exploded? The gas smell was getting stronger. Hopefully it wasn't leaking through the front windows to the spot on the porch where I'd left Ella. Spurred by that concern, I bent down to frantically claw at the ribbons around my ankles.

The door opened, allowing a sliver of light into the room.

"Jill!" someone whispered loudly. Desi. Why was she here?

"Desi, Ella's on the front porch. Be careful, the whole place is filling with gas."

"Ella's safe." She flung open the door and rushed in, opening the back door and other windows as quickly as possible to allow fresh air to circulate and gas to escape.

"It was Sandy," I said. "She's crazy." I glanced at Dorinda. Tears were streaming down her face.

Desi nodded grimly. "I saw her leave. I've called the

police. They'll be here soon, but we've got to get you both out of here." She eyed our bound appendages. "Jill, do you think you can walk?"

I stared at my feet. Sandy had tied them crossed, so I couldn't even hop out of the house. "I don't think so. I might be able to inchworm across the floor, but that's it."

"There's scissors in the knife block on the kitchen counter. You can use those to cut the ribbon," Dorinda said.

Desi ran into the kitchen. Drawers opened and shut with a bang, reminding me of the ignition device.

"Sandy set something up in there to light the gas," I shouted toward the kitchen.

The noises stopped. "Ok."

A minute later, Desi came running out with an extension cord and timer and threw it into the yard. She disappeared back into the kitchen and rushed out to us carrying scissors. Bizarrely, I couldn't help but want to advise her not to run with scissors, like she was a preschooler in danger.

"She broke the gas line to the stove. I can't turn it off. We've got to get out of here." She sliced through the ties on my feet and then freed Dorinda. The three of us ran for the door. From down the street came the telltale blare of sirens and approaching fire trucks.

We burst out of the house, running down the front walk and not stopping until we'd reached the sidewalk.

20

I turned to Desi, breathing heavily from the sudden exertion. "Where's Ella?"

She took my hand and led me across the street to a cute white house with blooming gardens out front. "One of Dorinda's neighbors was outside gardening, and I left Ella with her."

Sure enough, my daughter sat in an elderly woman's arms, cooing away. My heart surged with love. I'd come close to losing both my life and Ella's, and I wanted nothing more than to wrap my arms around my baby.

I held out my arms to the woman. "Thank you so much for watching my daughter."

She handed her to me, her lips spreading into a small smile. "No problem. I watch my great-granddaughter a few days a week, and I love babies. She and I have been doing fine."

I thanked her again, and Desi and I re-crossed the street to stand by the police cars, which were now blocking access to the area. Dorinda rushed over to us.

"They shut off the gas to the house, and the fire crew said the situation is safe now."

"Did they find Sandy?" Desi asked.

"I don't know," Dorinda replied.

A young, male police officer I'd never seen before approached us. "Excuse me, which of you were in the house with Ms. Lang?"

"I was." I stepped forward.

"I need to ask you a few questions." He got out his notebook and proceeded to quiz me on why I'd been at the residence and what had happened. When I finished, he thanked me for my time and walked over to an older man who I assumed was his superior at the police department.

Desi, Dorinda, Ella, and I huddled together near the street corner as the police and fire department activity buzzed around us. I shivered despite the warm June sun. "That was horrible." I'd been in danger before, but having the life of my daughter threatened was ten times worse. The police called Dorinda over to them. After she left, I turned to my sister-in-law.

"Desi, why were you here in the first place?" If she hadn't arrived when she had, we may not all have been standing there, safely watching the house from a distance.

"Uh, you're welcome?" she joked, and then seemed to catch the seriousness in my expression. "You left the aviator helmet behind at the café."

"I did? It must have fallen out of my hobo bag." With the bulky child carrier, I probably could have dropped a bowling ball from my bag and not noticed.

She shrugged. "Good thing you did. I found it when I was clearing the table and, after I closed up the café for the day, I decided to take it over to Dorinda's house before I forgot."

"How did you know where she lived?" I didn't think Desi had ever been to her house before.

With a chortle, Desi said, "Thank goodness for Nancy's organizational skills. She'd sent out an updated parent directory soon after Daniel started at the preschool. Dorinda's address was on it."

"Wow." I narrowed my eyes at her. "So you're saying Nancy basically saved us."

"Kind of." We exchanged glances.

"Let's not tell her, ok?" Nancy had a big enough head as it was, and I didn't want her to think I owed her.

"Deal. Besides, she'll be mad enough about someone in her perfect family being involved with such a public incident."

"Oh yeah. That's not going to go over well with her." I eyed the police officers, who were still interviewing Dorinda. "I'm going to check and see if it's ok if we leave. It's past the time I was supposed to meet my parents for dinner, and they'll be worried that I didn't show up."

My car was blocked in by emergency vehicles, with the side door open, revealing the giant airplane still inside.

"I want this thing out," I said to Desi. "And I never want to see it again. If I hadn't brought this over to Dorinda, I wouldn't have had to go through this."

"But what would have happened to her then?" Desi pointed out.

"You're right." I swear the nose of the airplane seemed to smile at me. "Still, can you help me move this over to the porch?"

"Sure. Do you want a ride home afterward?" She tipped her chin at the emergency vehicles surrounding my car.

"Yes, thank you." We wiggled the airplane out and set it on the lawn.

Dorinda walked up the sidewalk and nodded toward the airplane. "Thanks. I'll have someone help me get it inside when I get the all clear." She hugged me and then Desi. "And thank you both for being there for me." She shuddered. "If you hadn't been there, who knows what would have happened."

"Let us know if you need anything else, ok?"

"I will. Thank you again." Dorinda ran her hand over the airplane's smooth metal surface. "It feels good to have friends in town." Tears appeared in her eyes, and I patted her arm.

"I have to go, but I'll check in on you later when I come for my van."

She nodded and waved as Desi and I walked toward her car. In the car, Desi turned on the air conditioning, blasting us with cool air.

"Are you ok?" she asked.

"Yeah, I'm fine. I just never want to go through that again."

"No kidding," she said. "You both stayed so cool. I was freaked out."

"You did great. If it hadn't been for you, Dorinda, Ella, and I would be dead." My stomach clenched.

"How did you know something was wrong?"

"I got to Dorinda's house, and I saw your minivan outside with the door open, but you weren't around." Her knuckles were white on the steering wheel. "When I got up on the porch and saw Ella out there alone, I knew something was wrong. I peeked through the window and saw someone waving a gun around, so I grabbed Ella and called the police from across the street."

"You didn't have to come back for us. It would have been safer to stay there."

"I know," she said quietly. "But I couldn't leave you alone with that nut job. I went around to the back and saw her leave through the alley, so I knew it was safe to come in."

"Not really, we could have all blown up."

She pulled up to my house. My parent's car was in the driveway.

"I wasn't thinking about the danger. I just knew I had to do something."

I reached over the center console and hugged her tightly. "Thank you," I whispered. "Thank you so much."

She patted my back. "That's what friends are for."

I smiled at her and got myself and Ella out of the car, waving at Desi as she backed out of the driveway.

Wiping tears away from my eyes, I climbed the few steps to my front door and unlocked it. Before I could get the door open, I heard little feet pounding toward the door. I pushed it open gently so as not to hit Mikey.

"Mommy!" he shouted and launched himself into my arms. I leaned down to hug him, squeezing him tighter than normal. He didn't seem to mind.

"You didn't come home for dinner, and Grandma said you were delayed. What does delayed mean? Is it bad?"

I peered into his face and ruffled his hair. "No, honey, I'm fine. Delayed means something made me late."

His face erupted into a smile. "Ok. Hey, Grandma made a blackberry cobbler. You should try it, it's yummy!" He ran off toward the kitchen, brushing past my mom, who was making her way to the front door.

I moved Ella's carrier inside. She smiled and blew bubbles at me, completely unfazed by the day's events. I picked her up and snuggled her close.

"Do you want me to take her?" Mom asked.

"No, I'll hold her. Thanks." I smiled at her.

"What happened today?" she whispered.

I glanced at Mikey, chattering away to his grandfather. I didn't want him to overhear if I told my mother. "I'll tell you later," I whispered back.

She caught me checking on Mikey and nodded. We walked together into the kitchen, where she served me a plate full of food. I placed Ella in her high chair and put some mashed carrots and a small portion of meatloaf on the tray in front of her. Mikey and my parents finished their dessert while I ate dinner. Looking around the table, I saw such a peaceful scene that I could almost forget the terror I'd felt when Sandy held a gun on me at Dorinda's house.

I set my fork down. Sandy. Had they caught her? I suddenly felt a sense of unease.

"Mom? I'm going to make a quick phone call."

She looked at me with concern but nodded.

I went down the hall and pulled my cell phone out of my pocket. Desi answered the call on the second ring.

"Desi. Did they catch Sandy? I can't focus on anything knowing she could still be out there." My eyes darted to the window, as if Sandy was lurking close by outside.

"Tomàs just told me they arrested her at her house. She acted like nothing had happened and that we were crazy. I was about to call you when my phone rang."

I breathed a huge sigh of relief. "Thank goodness. I'd better get back to the kids and my parents, but I had to know. Goodnight. I'll see you tomorrow, ok?"

"See you."

She hung up, and I slowly put the phone back in my pocket. This wasn't exactly what I'd intended when I vowed to help Brenda by finding out who had killed Louis Mahoney, but we were all safe, and everything had turned out ok.

I plastered a smile on my face and returned to the dinner table.

"Everything ok?" my dad asked.

"Yep, everything's fine."

I'm sure it would be in a few days, but until then, I'd have to fake it. I never wanted them to know how close I'd come to death.

21

The next morning, Adam was home, and I filled him in on what had happened at Dorinda's house while he filled his travel coffee mug from the carafe.

"You could have been killed." He set down the cream he'd been pouring in his coffee and stared at me.

"I know." The icy fear shot through my body again. I knew from past experience that for a while, every time I thought about what happened, I would relive it. I only hoped that it would pass quickly. "But I wasn't. I'm fine, Ella's fine."

He wrapped his arms around me, looking into my eyes. "You need a break."

"Right. I know. But that's never going to happen." Although the auction was over, I still had my job, my family, and everything else I was responsible for. A break was a far-off dream for the future.

"Eh, it might be closer than you think," he said mysteriously. He kissed me atop my head. "See you after work."

I watched his car pull out of the driveway. What had he

meant by a break being closer than I'd think? Excitement rose in my chest. Would we someday get to go on that couples vacation I'd been dreaming of?

I'd gone through this before and only experienced disappointment when our vacation plans had turned into a camping trip with the kids—that I was in charge of planning. For once, I wanted someone to plan a vacation, preferably somewhere tropical, and tell me when and where to show up. With a husband as busy as Adam, though, it wasn't going to happen anytime soon.

My parents surprised me by asking to take Ella and Mikey out on a day trip to Pike Place Market and the Seattle waterfront, leaving me free to catch up on some work that I'd put off in the auction crunch. When that was finished, I met Desi for lunch at Elmer's Sea of Fish.

We took our fried cod and chips to the beach and straddled a beach log facing each other to eat. I propped my large iced tea up in a small indentation in the gnarled wood.

"You don't look so good," Desi said.

"Well, I did have a gun pointed at me yesterday." I glared at her. The truth was, I'd had nightmares about a crazed Sandy all night and hadn't slept well.

"Yeah." She gazed out at Puget Sound. "Next time, let's leave any sleuthing to the police."

"Hey, it wasn't even my investigation that got me in that mess."

"You said Sandy knew we'd been in her house and that we'd told the police about the photos of her husband with other women."

I made a face. She had a point. "You're the one who wanted to bring her a casserole so we could snoop."

Desi grinned and held up her hands in front of her face.

"I know, I know." Her expression darkened. "I've never been so scared as when I saw Ella sitting there alone on the porch and then saw you and Dorinda on the couch with your hands and feet bound when I peeked in the window. I don't want to do that again."

"No sleuthing for us ever again, agreed?" I held out my hand and she shook it.

"Deal."

We polished off our food and stuffed the wrappers into the paper sack from Elmer's. I slurped my iced tea and willed my mind to relax. The waves lapping at the shore did little to soothe the activity in my brain. What had Adam been hinting about that morning?

"Adam mentioned something about taking a break. Has he said anything to you about a vacation?"

She suddenly became very interested in her soft drink cup, drawing designs in the condensation.

"Desi ... do you know something?"

She looked up but avoided my gaze. "Maybe he's going to quit his job soon?"

I narrowed my eyes at her. "No, that's not the impression I got."

She shrugged and hopped off the log. "I don't talk to him much."

I noticed she hadn't answered my question, but I dropped the line of inquisition. "Are you sending Anthony to summer camp at Busy Bees?"

"Yes, he'll have the same schedule as usual. Mikey?"

I nodded. "I think he'll go most weeks this summer. He's too active to keep with me at the Boathouse on a regular basis, and I think he'll have more fun with friends. It'll be weird to not be with him during the days this summer though."

"I was talking with Tomàs about going camping, maybe in August. Do you guys want to come?"

"Sounds fun. I'll see if Adam can get the time off."

"So *has* he said anything lately about quitting?" Desi sucked her drink down until air bubbles crackled through the plastic straw.

I jumped down onto the soft sand, which shifted under the rubber soles of my sandals. I brushed the sand off the backs of my legs and picked up the remains of our lunch from the log.

"He hasn't said anything." I looked out at the calm seas. The salty air filled my lungs, invigorating me. I turned to Desi and stared into her eyes. "I'm going to ask him tonight. He needs to make a decision about his job soon. I can't take this indecisiveness anymore."

"Good for you." She smiled. "Sometimes he needs a nudge to make a big jump."

"Yeah, I guess so." I'd always thought of my husband as being a strong decision-maker, but in reality, he'd gone from college straight into this job. He'd never really tried anything else. For the sake of our family and his own sanity, he'd decided to branch out on his own with a small private practice to be opened in Ericksville. But to do that, he needed to quit his old job.

After saying goodbye to Desi, I went home and made a list of everything I could think of that Adam would need to do to set up a new business. When I finished, I could see why he felt overwhelmed by the task, but I was determined to make this work for our family. I printed out a list of commercial real estate spaces in downtown Ericksville and information about the necessary licenses and insurance that he'd need. Then, my enthusiasm deflated, and I settled down on the couch in front of the TV, watching reruns of a sitcom until Adam came home.

"Hey, honey," he said, setting his messenger bag down on the recliner. "Busy day?" He motioned to me lying on the couch and raised his eyebrows.

I rose hastily. "I was so tired after everything that I couldn't do anything else until I'd rested for a while."

He smiled and came over to stand in front of me, resting his hands on my shoulders. "I wasn't being critical. You deserve some time off. In fact, you need more than just an afternoon of TV." He stared into my eyes. "How would you feel about a week in Jamaica?"

"That would be awesome, but it's never going to happen with the kids and our work schedules." The enormity of everything that would need to slip into place to have a couple's vacation hit me, making me more weary than I'd been before.

"It's all taken care of." He walked over to his bag and retrieved a brochure that matched the one I'd found in the mail. "We leave on Saturday."

My eyes bugged out. "You're kidding. Saturday? As in four days from now?" I leaned back into the couch, filled with a mix of exhilaration and apprehension. "Who's watching the kids?"

"Your parents are going to stay here to watch them together," he said smoothly.

"But I have responsibilities at the Boathouse," I protested. "I can't leave your parents hanging." I did like the idea of my parents spending time together in a different environment from their house. It might have been a little *Parent Trap*-ish, but I still had hope that they'd decide to stay together.

"Who do you think helped put me in touch with the

travel agency I booked through? My mom recommended an old friend of hers over on Grand Avenue in Everton."

That location sounded familiar. Grand Avenue was where Adam had received the red light camera ticket. Relief flooded through me. I knew he hadn't cheated on me, but there was still a little part of me that had been concerned about what he'd been doing in that part of town.

"So Beth is taking over for me next week?"

He nodded. "She is. And Desi said she'd help out if they needed it." He leaned in to me. "Honey, you need a vacation."

"But what about your job? Will they let you take this time off?"

"I have weeks of vacation saved up. They were fine with it."

I remembered the lists I'd made earlier. "Have you thought any more about quitting your job?"

Adam sighed. "I have. I even looked at a few office spaces in Ericksville, but I haven't found the right location yet."

I went to my desk and brought back the lists and print-outs I'd prepared. "I know it's overwhelming, but we can work on it together, ok?" I gave him a chance to review the documents.

He scanned them and then lifted his head, relief discernible in his features. "Thanks. When we get back from vacation, I'll take a closer look at these. I'm going to take a few extra days off after we get back. Maybe I can knock off some of these tasks then."

Tears came to my eyes. Maybe his career change would become a reality sometime in the near future.

"Great," I said. "Now, let's get packing for that trip. I can't wait to relax on the beach without a little hand grabbing me to ask for another cup of juice. Are you sure we can't leave today?"

Laughing, he led me to the stairs and we went up to our bedroom together to start packing and getting a head start on our romantic couples-only vacation. For the first time in weeks, I felt truly hopeful about the future and more than a little excited for a week of fun in the sun. It was more than I could have dreamed about.

22

The next day, I brought the auction proceeds check with me when I picked up Mikey from preschool. There was no getting around it. I had to see Nancy to give her the check. Buoyed by the thought of my upcoming vacation, the thought of seeing her didn't bother me nearly as much as it usually would.

Outside, the sun shone brightly, glinting off the steeple of the Lutheran church a few blocks away, and a slight breeze kicked up the scent of the flower bushes blooming next to the door to Busy Bees Preschool. I'd had a productive day at work and was filled with optimism for the future.

Parents were showing up to check their kids out of school, and I had to weave my way through a teeming mass of children and adults to get through the lobby. I stuck my head into Mikey's classroom, but his teacher was still reading them a story, so I opted to find Nancy before getting him. I passed by Sugar and Spice's terrarium and had a fleeting thought that maybe they weren't too bad. Should I let Mikey take them home? I stared at them and then thought better of it. My newfound bright outlook on life didn't extend to allowing rodents in my house.

I traveled down the hallway, glancing into every room. There was no sign of Nancy. Had she not come in to volunteer that day? Busy Bees was her life, and I wasn't sure what she'd do when her youngest daughter aged out of the school after pre-kindergarten the next year.

In a darkened classroom, I found her. She was sitting on a stool leaning against the wall, crying. She blew her nose loudly. As I approached, she quickly stood and smoothed her skirt.

"Nancy? Is that you?" I called out, acting as if I didn't know it was her.

"You're not supposed to be back here. This classroom is closed up for the day."

I took a step back, out of the room. Given the circumstances, I'd give her the joy of telling me what to do for once.

"Sorry. I was looking for you, and I thought I heard someone back here." I inched further into the hallway. "I have the auction check for you. I'll meet you in Ms. Shana's classroom, ok?"

"Yes. I will see you in a few minutes." She sniffled, almost imperceptibly. I hurried away. I wasn't sure how she'd react to having been seen in a weakened state.

I hung out at the back of Mikey's classroom for several minutes before Nancy appeared. Her eyes were rimmed with red, but she'd regained her composure.

"So you're here with the check?" Her eagle eyes assessed me.

I nodded. "I think you'll be happy with the total. The parents were quite generous this year."

"Well, I can't imagine why," she grumbled. "The Boathouse was a disgrace."

I bit my tongue to keep from lashing out at her. She had the power to make Mikey's life and mine miserable. "I'm sorry you feel that way." I held out the check. "Anyways, here you go."

She plucked it roughly from my hand and tore it out of the envelope. "I suppose this wasn't too bad, given the circumstances."

I resisted her dig. "The preschool should be able to afford those special computers they wanted to order for the kids. Won't that be great?"

"Well. I don't know about that. I'm not sure this will cover it. But maybe." She stuffed the check back into the envelope for safekeeping. "You'll have to do better next year. We want to get new playground equipment, including a climbing toy and a playhouse."

I stared at her. "Did you say next year?"

"Well, yes. I'm sure you'll want to make up for the debacle this year with a better effort next year, right?" She said all of this while looking down her nose at me.

I floundered for the right words to say. "I thought you hated having it at the Boathouse?"

"Well, it is close and probably the best we can do with our budget. Of course, if we could afford something better, we would."

"Of course." My teeth were clenched so hard I was thinking again about visiting the dentist. "We'll see about next year."

Nancy looked at her watch. "You're three minutes late to pick up Mikey."

I raised my eyebrows and started to speak, then thought better of it. "I'll pick him up right now. Have a nice day."

I swiveled on my heel and rushed away from her as fast as I could without breaking into a run. I grabbed Mikey and his backpack, signed him out, and left. If I saw Nancy again, I'd probably tell her off, and I wanted to keep the peace, no matter how much I disliked her.

23

"I know it's not much, but I wanted to give you something to thank you for believing in me." Brenda set one of her Watkins Real Estate gift baskets on my desk.

Bile rose in my throat, but I forced it back and pasted a smile on my face.

"Thank you so much. Adam and I will enjoy the wine and chocolates." I stood from my desk chair and walked over to her, giving her a quick hug. "And I knew you hadn't done it. You don't have it in you to kill someone."

"Well, maybe my ex-husband ..." she joked. Then she sobered. "I probably shouldn't say that. If something happened to him, I'd feel bad, even with all of our differences."

"Did he decide to take that job out-of-town? That would be rough on Dara and Sara to not see him very often."

"No, he decided to stay here. He really does want to be a big part of their lives, and I think we're going to keep our existing custody arrangement since we live so close."

"Good. I'm happy for you." I gave her another hug.

"Me too." She scanned the room. "Hey, did you do something with your office? It looks nice."

"I did." I beamed with pride. "The desk and rug are new, and I hung up some of Mikey's artwork." Beth had given me a small allowance to redecorate, and I'd found a white Ikea desk and turquoise rug to liven up the dark space. I'd also framed some of Mikey's crayon drawings in white wooden frames. With a small investment, the office now felt like mine.

"Well, it looks great." She smiled at me. "And I should get back to my own work. With everything going on, I've neglected some of my clients. Have fun on your trip with Adam."

"I will."

Brenda left, and I sat back down in my chair to survey the room. Yes, it definitely felt like my office now and not an impersonal office given to a transient employee. The success of the auction had buoyed my spirits and made me realize how much I loved my new job at the Boathouse. Even so, I was excited about my upcoming couples-only trip to Jamaica with Adam.

A week later, I was lying on a white sandy beach in Jamaica, wondering how I was ever going to go back to Ericksville. I knew we'd have to leave in a few days, and I was starting to miss the kids a bit, but for now, I was enjoying relaxing and spending some well-deserved alone time with my husband.

I looked over to Adam, who sat reading a book in a white lounge chair next to me. I hadn't seen him this content in a long time. Usually, he had his eyes glued to his work laptop or his ears connected to his cell phone. Having him open his own practice in Ericksville wouldn't be easy for us in the beginning, financially or otherwise, but I knew having him get away from working and traveling so much would be the best thing for our family.

He saw me looking and smiled at me. "Are you ready for another drink?"

I stared down at the dregs of my piña colada. "Yes, definitely."

"Do you want to check out the swim-up bar?"

I thought about the crowds at the pool. "No, but how about we get drinks at the bar and take them back to our room? We can order room service and pretend like we're the only people here."

His smile widened, and his blue eyes danced. "I like how you think."

He grabbed my hand, and we walked off toward the bar at the edge of the beach. As the sun warmed my skin and the sand filtered through my toes, I glanced up at his face and knew that although our life may not always be fun in the sun, we'd always have each other and could work through anything that might come our way.

FROM THE AUTHOR

Thank you for reading the second book in the Jill Andrews Cozy Mystery series. I've loved writing this series and I hope to write more.

I'm writing a few series at the moment and as a book's success is partially based on reviews, if you'd like me to write more in this series, I'd love it if you'd leave a review on Amazon. Thank you!

Other books in this series
    Brownie Points for Murder (Book 1)
    A Deadly Pair O'Docks (Book 3)
    - coming May 15th, 2018
    Available on Amazon and Kindle Unlimited

Candle Beach Sweet Romance series
    Sweet Beginnings (Book 1)
    Sweet Success (Book 2)

From the Author

Sweet Promises (Book 3)
Sweet Memories (Book 4)
Available on Amazon and Kindle Unlimited